T0161953

THE DAO IN ACTION

My love of fables began when I was very young. Many of the stories my mother and my White Crane master told me have guided my Dao.

—Dr. Yang, Jwing-Ming

THE DAO IN ACTION

Inspired Tales for Life

Dr. Yang, Jwing-Ming

YMAA Publication Center
Wolfeboro, New Hampshire

YMAA Publication Center, Inc.
PO Box 480
Wolfeboro, New Hampshire, 03894
1-800-669-8892 • info@ymaa.com • www.ymaa.com

ISBN: 9781594396519 (print) • ISBN: 9781594396526 (ebook)

Cover design: Axie Breen
Illustrations: F. L. Walker
Editor: Leslie Takao
Proofreader: Doran Hunter
Managing editor: T. G. LaFredo
This book typeset in Electra LT

10 9 8 7 6 5 4 3 2 1

Publisher's Cataloging in Publication

Names: Yang, Jwing-Ming, 1946-
Title: The dao in action : inspired tales for life / by Dr. Yang, Jwing-Ming.
Description: Wolfeboro, NH USA : YMAA Publication Center, [2019]
Identifiers: ISBN: 9781594396519 (print) | 9781594396526 (ebook) |
    LCCN: 2019931196
Subjects: LCSH: Martial arts—Philosophy. | Martial arts—Parables.
    | Martial arts—Moral and ethical aspects. | Tao. | Taoist parables. | Taoist
    philosophy. | Yin-yang—Parables. | Conduct of life—Parables. | Integrity—
    Parables. | Inspiration—Parables. | Ethics—Parables. | Kindness—
    Parables. | Perseverance (Ethics)—Parables. | LCGFT: Fables. |
    Exempla. | BISAC: SPORTS & RECREATION / Martial Arts &
    Self-Defense. | BODY, MIND & SPIRIT / Inspiration &
    Personal Growth. | PHILOSOPHY / Ethics & Moral Philosophy.
    | PHILOSOPHY / Taoist. | LITERARY COLLECTIONS /
    Asian / Chinese.
Classification: LCC: GV1102.7.M67 Y36 2019 | DDC: 796.8—dc23

Printed in Canada.

Dedications
To my grandma (楊葉端);
my White Crane master (曾金灶); and
my grandchildren, Jayden (楊傑龍) and
Mikayla (楊思宇)
—and to the child's heart in everyone.

Acknowledgements

First, I would like to thank Dr. Robert J. Woodbine, who put in a lot of effort editing my "Chinglish." I would also like to thank Mr. David Silver for his foreword, Ms. Leslie Takao for her editing and her foreword, Mr. T. G. LaFredo for his editing, and Mr. Frank Walker for his illustrations.

Finally, I would like to express my gratitude to those who have listened to my stories in the past. It was their interest and encouragement that inspired me to compile these stories and share them with more people.

Foreword by Leslie Takao

I love these stories. Some are inspirational, some are funny, and some are thought provoking. Many of you will recognize the themes of these fables. You may have heard them with other names and places. The themes, noble and ignoble, transcend culture and time. The Dao is the Dao, and fables are the *de* (the manifestations) of the Dao.

In the last hours of the last days of many of Master Yang's seminars, when we were physically drained from training and mentally void from trying to remember new forms and new skills, Master Yang would sit down, answer questions, and tell stories. Sometimes, during regular classes, he would tell one of these stories to make a point. These were my favorite times; time to get to know our teacher and to absorb an important spiritual and inspirational part of the training. I find myself often retelling many of these stories to my students.

I would like to add my own story. Once upon a time, in real life, my mother was a civilian worker at the US naval base in Pearl Harbor, Hawaii, during World War II. It was not a top-secret area; we are Japanese. There was a prisoner of war, a Japanese national, who was allowed to clean the offices where she worked. She would sometimes offer this man a stick of gum or share some of the Japanese food she had brought for lunch, little kindnesses to which she gave no second thought. She never even mentioned them to us.

If the story ended here, it would just be a story about a kind lady. But the story does not end here.

It ends about forty years later when the Japanese embassy contacted my mother. That prisoner of war had gone on to become a successful CEO of a large sake company, and he had been looking for my mother for several years. He wanted to thank her. To him, her gestures were not just small kindnesses; they made him feel like a human being again and reinstilled in him the will to live. He sent her two first-class tickets to Japan and treated her and my father like royalty.

The consequence of her small actions was the profound change in the course of another human life. That consequence honors her otherwise ordinary human gestures. That is the ethos of a fable.

These fables of human integrity, kindness, perseverance, wonder, and honor are the revelations of the Dao. Read them in order or randomly. Most of all, enjoy.

Foreword by David Silver

Throughout his many years of teaching in his Boston YMAA head-quarters school, in classes around the world, and more recently at the YMAA Retreat Center, Dr. Yang has always incorporated fables and proverbs. While we were building the retreat center, and during his years teaching there, Dr. Yang scheduled a "story time" at the end of each day so he could tell us these old tales and then discuss their deeper meaning.

I have heard a number of these fables over the years and fondly recall Dr. Yang's zeal in sharing and discussing them. He always had a sparkle in his eye as he reminisced about these life lessons handed down from his mother and teachers. That same passion to help others find deeper meaning shines through in this book. What astounds me is how many of these tales I have never heard over the past decades and how many more Dr. Yang has known but has not shared until now!

A fun aspect of this book is that within its pages are several stories Dr. Yang has written himself based on his personal experiences. This collection offers a rare insight into another side of Dr. Yang's personality and teaching that gives readers everywhere a chance to get to know him (and themselves) a little better.

Table of Contents

Acknowledgements . . . . *vii*

Foreword by Leslie Takao . . . . *ix*

Foreword by David Silver. . . . . *xi*

The Taller the Bamboo Grows, the Lower It Bows. 1

Carry a Heavy Bucket. 3

The Engineer Serves Coffee. 3

One Plus One Does Not Equal Two 4

Revenge on a Classmate. 5

Pick Up a Paper Napkin from the Floor 6

The Attitude of Learning Gongfu 7

The Mind of Wonders 9

Happiness Recovered. 10

Two Monks and a Lady 11

A Blessing in Disguise 13

Two Tigers. 14

A Bowl of Example. 15

A Bowl of Noodle Soup 17

A Donkey, a Father, and a Son 18

A Farmer Buys His Shoes 19

A Fight of No Fight 20

A New Lake for the Old .24

A Rich Man in Jail 25

The Man Only Saw Gold 26

An Attorney's Only Son .26

An Untrustworthy Wolf .29

Arrogance Will Be Defeated 30

A Beacon Destroys a Country 32

Beijing Doll Maker 33

Boiling a Pot of Water 34

Break the Cistern to Save a Friend 36

The Buddha Crosses the River 36

Buying a Good Horse 37

Fishing with a Carrot 38

Carry Thorns to Request Forgiveness 38

Carving a Buddha 41

Clay Image and Wooden Image 45

Clench the Fist Tightly 46

Confucius Learns the Chinese Zither 47

Cooking the Hounds Once the Hares Are Caught 48

Cover the Ears to Steal the Bell 50

Dawn Three and Dusk Four 50

Different Paths 51

Divine Fish in a Maple Tree 52

Disguise of Two Myopics .53

Doomsday of Cuttlefish 53

The Dragon and the Local Snake 54

Drawing a Snake with Legs 55

Dream of Cooking the Goose 56

Becoming Rich with an Egg 57

False Dignity Gets Its Reward 57
Foolish Old Man Moves the Mountain 62
One Perfect Kick 63
Good Retribution of a Kind Heart .63
Sharing Food in Heaven and Hell 66
Greediness Gets Its Reward 67
Grind the Steel Rod into a Needle .70
Hard to Be a Good Person 71
Hear and Talk on the Way 72
Help the Rice to Grow 72
Hou Yi Learns Archery 73
Learn What to Pick Up 77
Learning Patience 78
The Final Goal of Practicing Archery 79
Lost Sheep in Many Paths 81
Mark the Boat to Find the Sword .82
Money Is More Important Than Life 83
The Mother of Mencius Breaks the Loom 84
The Mother of Mencius Moves Three Times 84
No Dregs for the Swine 85
No More Space 86
Nonsense of Flattering 88
Stubbornly Mistaken 88
One Bowl of Rice 89
Painting Ghosts Is Easiest 91
Praying Mantis Seizes the Cicadas .91
Presenting Doves for the New Year 92
Pretending to Be an Expert on Reed Pipes 93
Qi Xi Requests Retirement 94
A Raven and a Rabbit 95

River Deity Gets Married .95

Seven People Share Rice Soup 99

Shu Zhan Saves the Country 100

Snake Shadow on the Cup 101

Spears and Shields against Each Other 103

Strange Human Thinking 103

Swearing In a Corrupt Official 104

The Borderline of Life and Death 104

The Broken Wall 105

The Carp in the Dry Track 105

The Cat and the Tiger 106

The Conceited Carriage Coachman 109

The Cunning of a Student 110

A Broken Porcelain Bowl 111

The Wisdom of a Child 113

The Wisdom of Another Child 113

The Donkey Lover 114

The End of the Guizhou Donkey 114

The Feeling of a General 116

The Fight of the Snipe and the Mussel 116

The Fox Borrows the Tiger's Awe 117

The Hunter's Fate 119

The Innocent Fawn 120

The Lamb in Tiger Skin 121

The Lord of Yan Looking for Longevity 121

The Lord Who Loved Dragons 122

The Lost Ax 122

The Love of the Kingfisher 122

The Owl Moves His Home 123

The Poison of Love 123

The Repentance of an Old Man 126
The Retribution of the Merchant 127
The Thief and the Bell 129
The Mask of the King 131
The Value of a Horse 132
The Warning of a Wild Goose Sentry 133
Three Metaphors on Study 134
Three Monks 135
Two Children Discuss the Sun 137
Wipe Windows for Five Years 138
Zeng Shen Kills Someone 139
Zeng Shen Kills the Pig 140
Zhang, San-Feng Teaches Taiji Sword 141
Zou Ji Compares His Beauty 142
Thirty Years of More Mistakes 143
The Trick of Gold 143
A Master's Answer 144
Two Make One 145
A Swordsman's Revenge 145
Bai-Yin the Monk 148
Destiny of Coin Tossing 150
The Full Cup 150
Heaven and Hell 152
A Lesson to the Prince 153
Big Rocks in a Jar 154
Pipeline in Life 157
A Businessman 158
A Child Crosses the Street 158
A Cup of Poison 159
A Dog and a Wolf 160

A Driver and a Policeman. 161
A Forgotten Regret. 161
A Glass 162
A Happy Servant 162
A Hound and a Rabbit 163
A Performer and His Assistant. 163
A Reward for Kindness 165
A Rich Man and His Mother 166
A Spider in the Web. 167
A Change of Fortune 167
A Weasel and a Lion. 169
A Wise Man and Two Hungry People 169
A Prayer's Request 170
An Ocean Fish Drowns in a Creek 170
An Old Companionship. 172
An Old Man Loses His Shoe 173
Annoying Disturbance 174
Body of Millions of Dollars. 174
Buying a Puppy 175
Catch One Each Time. 176
Choosing a Wife 177
Friend and Enemy. 177
God's Gift 178
Good Marriage 178
Increase the Height of the Fence 179
Losing Money 179
Lucky Table. 181
New Year's Present. 182
Dream Come True 184
Paid by the Sound of a Coin. 184

Priest's Prayer on the Roof 185
Psychological Healing 186
Plot against Plot 186
Retirement of an Old Carpenter 187
Selling Milk 187
The Contented Fisherman 188
The Dog and the Reflection 188
The Love of a Child 190
The Love of a Few Dollars 191
The Unhappy Barber 193
Three Small Devils 194
Two Escaping Mice 195
Two Mice in a Milk Pot 197
Two Radio Stations 198
A Frog in the Well 198
The Wisdom of a Wise Old Man 200

About the Author 203

The Taller the Bamboo Grows, the Lower It Bows

This is a story my White Crane master told me when I was seventeen.

Once there was a bamboo shoot that had just popped up out of the ground. It looked at the sky and smiled. It said to itself, "Someone told me that the sky is so high that it cannot be reached. I don't believe that's true."

The sprout was young and felt strong. It believed if it kept growing, one day it could reach the sky. So it kept growing and growing. Ten years passed. Twenty years passed. Again it looked at the sky. The sky was still very high, and it was still far beyond the bamboo's reach. Finally, it realized something and started to bow. The more it grew the lower it bowed.

My teacher said, "Remember, the taller the bamboo grows, the lower it bows." The Chinese people also have a saying: "Satisfaction loses and humility gains." The Daoists say, "In order to fill up the room, first you must empty your mind."

Carry a Heavy Bucket

One day, my White Crane master said to us, "There are ten buckets of water. Some are empty, some are half full, and some are completely full." He asked, "If you have a choice to carry one bucket to my rice field, which one do you prefer?"

Some of my classmates said, "I will carry an empty one."

Another felt somewhat bad if he said he would carry an empty one, so he said, "I will choose the half-full one."

Only a couple of students said, "I will carry the full bucket."

My master smiled and said, "Those who carry the full bucket will have a chance to condition their body, and those who choose easy ones will miss the opportunity." The Chinese have a saying: "When carrying a load, choose a heavy load. When climbing the mountain, choose a high mountain to climb." (挑擔要找重擔挑，爬山要找高山爬。)

The Engineer Serves Coffee

There was a Chinese man who earned a PhD in engineering. With his advanced degree he quickly found an engineering job, and he was very happy. On the first day at work, he discovered his boss did not like "the short Chinese young guy." His boss had graduated with a BS degree and had been working for this company for more than thirty years. The Chinese engineer had graduated with a PhD from a well-known university. When this Chinese engineer reported to work in his boss's office, the boss said, "Now you report to me, so you have to listen to me. I want you to bring me a cup of black coffee every morning before you begin your other work. Understand?"

"Yes, sir," he said. "I will bring you a cup of black coffee every morning." Though he knew bringing coffee for his boss was not his duty, he did not argue with his boss. He was new and wanted to avoid creating a poor relationship.

So, he brought coffee to his boss every morning and worked very hard at his engineering job. After one year, he had established a good relationship with all the employees and earned the company's trust. Now, his boss began to feel guilty about abusing him.

One day, the boss told him, "OK. From tomorrow morning, you don't have to bring me coffee anymore."

The Chinese guy replied with a smile, "OK. From tomorrow morning, no more spit."

One Plus One Does Not Equal Two

This conversation opened my mind. Now, I believe the arts are creative and not dead.

After I trained White Crane for nearly one year, I discovered that, for the same movement, two of my older classmates applied it differently. I was confused and believed one movement should have only one application. I wanted to understand, so I went to ask my master.

Instead of answering my questions, he asked, "Little Yang, how much is one plus one?"

"Two, master." I said. I wondered why he asked this simple question.

"No, it is not two, little Yang."

"Master, one plus one is two. I know I am right." I was very confused.

"You see, little Yang, your father is one and your mother is one. After they got married, they had five children. Now, you see, one plus one is seven instead of two. If you treat an art like it's dead, it is two. But if you think the art is alive, it can be many. The arts are creative and, therefore, they can be many from derivation. Applications are derived from movement, so there are many."

Revenge on a Classmate

When I was learning gongfu from Master Cheng in 1963, one of my senior classmates was never fond of me. I don't know why. Maybe it was because I was new and the last student (the nineteenth) accepted by my master. Whatever the reason, this classmate did not like me. When I began my training and for the following two years, he always gave me trouble. He would kick me during training and a few times he even injured me intentionally. I had a feeling he wanted to force me out of the class. However, no matter what, I kept hanging in there.

Later I left my hometown, Xinzhu (新竹), to move to Taipei (台北) for my college studies at Tamkang University (淡江大學). I had the opportunity to learn Long Fist (長拳) gongfu from Master Li, Mao-Ching (李茂清). From Master Li, my skills advanced rapidly, especially long-range fighting.

A few days before my departure to the US for my PhD studies at Purdue University, I had a chance to visit my old classmate's school. He had been teaching for several years, and out of curiosity I went to visit his school.

When I arrived, he was teaching a bare-hand matching sequence. I proposed that it would be clearer if both of us could demonstrate how the sequence could be done. He agreed. When we demonstrated,

I began to speed up. My reactions were so quick that he was unable to block my strikes. I embarrassed him in front of his students. His face turned flushed, and I could tell he felt uneasy. I said my good-byes, and I left.

When I stepped outside his school, I felt great. In my early years of training this man was my senior classmate, and he had often intentionally injured me. For ten years I had carried my resentment, and I finally had the chance to release it. However, after I calmed down and thought it over, I began to feel ashamed. I felt I was small and had showed little magnanimity. I regretted what I had done and swore I would never do it again.

I remembered Master Cheng said, "When a dog bites you, you don't bite it back. Otherwise, what is the difference between you and the dog?" He also said, "You should train your temper and tolerance in such a way that even if someone spits in your face, you don't even bother to wipe it off but let it dry by itself." It is not easy to reach this level of tolerance.

Pick Up a Paper Napkin from the Floor

When I was in Boston, I taught a series of seminars twice per year. Often, I had more than fifty participants for each of my seminars. One winter I had a very good turnout for one of my seminars, nearly seventy participants.

On the first day of the seminar, early that morning, I went to Dunkin' Donuts to buy some donuts for the participants. After I purchased six dozen doughnuts, I also grabbed a pile of paper napkins. With my two hands full with donuts, one paper napkin dropped out of my hand onto the floor before I stepped out of the door. When I realized it, I thought, "It is inside of the donut shop; they will clean it up later." So, I continued to walk toward the door.

Before I reached the door, a portly lady stood right in front of me. She looked at me and said, "Pick it up!" She was serious.

"It is inside of the shop, and I believe they will clean it up soon." I looked at her with a smile.

"I don't care. Just pick it up," she insisted.

About twelve people in the shop noticed what was happening and looked at us, waiting to see what would happen next. I began to get upset and thought that my accidentally dropping the napkin was none of her business. Why was she so concerned about it? However, after a few seconds, I placed the donuts on the counter and picked up the paper napkin on the floor. After I threw it into the trash can, I faced her directly, looked at her eyes, and gave her a ninety-degree bow. I said, "Thank you very much, madam."

What I did shocked everyone in the shop since they were expecting a fight. I simply picked up the donuts and paper napkins and stepped out of the door.

After I stepped out the door, I smiled inside my heart. I said to myself, "This time, I conquered myself."

The Attitude of Learning Gongfu

During the 1960s, we began to see plastic objects, such as flowers or fruits, for the first time. One day, my White Crane master got us together. From his pocket, he took out an orange. He asked, "Do you know what this is?"

"It is an orange, master!" we all replied.

He laughed and said, "No! Actually, it is not. It is a piece of plastic." He handed the fake orange to us so we could see the truth.

Then, from his other pocket, he took out another orange. We all paid close attention to the orange this time and hoped not to be fooled again. He said, "Now, this is the real orange. Tell me, do you know what is this orange?"

"We know, master. We know it is an orange."

"OK. Then tell me if this orange is sweet or sour," he said.

"No, master! We don't know."

"Now you realize that seeing can, again, fool you," he said. Next, he peeled the orange and gave us one piece each. We all tasted it. He said again, "Now do you know the orange?"

"Master, we know now."

"No! You don't. If you really know the orange, please tell me how it grows. What kind of soil, sunshine, water, and fertilizer are required for growing an orange?"

Now we were all quiet since we did not know anything about growing oranges. Then he said, "You see! Learning gongfu is the same. Looking is not as real as feeling. And feeling is still not good enough to become an expert. To be an expert, you must know how to create instead of just learning and selling. The art is alive and created from deep feeling. If the feeling of creation is shallow, the art created will also be shallow."

Indeed, this short lesson has since influenced my attitude about learning.

The Mind of Wonders

After I had practiced White Crane gongfu for one year, I was saddened to find that, even though I tried so hard, I failed to make as much progress as my classmates. This sadness often influenced my practice.

One afternoon, after school, I went to my master's home and was happy to see he was available. Since I'd begun practicing gongfu, whenever I felt confused about my life or uncertain about decisions I had to make, I would go to see him for advice. I told my master that, compared to my classmates, I felt so stupid and slow in my practice.

He looked at me and said, "Little Yang! Why do you look around when you are learning or working? If you see you are ahead of others, you will be satisfied, and this will weaken your will for progressing. If you see you are behind, you will be discouraged and feel sorrow for yourself. The way to achieve success in your practice is just like plowing a field. Bow your head low and keep digging. Look only ahead of you, not sideways or even behind you. Simply keep digging and digging. Someday, only someday, after a long period of time, when you take a break and look around, you will suddenly realize there is nobody around you or near you simply because all of them have been left far behind you. A good harvest comes from hard work, not from comparison."

Since then, I have kept practicing, studying, and pondering ceaselessly, without ever worrying about the progress of other people. I did not comprehend the true results of this effort until I came to the United States and quit my engineering job, relying solely on gongfu for my living.

Happiness Recovered

When I was in France to teach seminars, there was a young man who had taken several of my previous seminars. One time his natural smile and happy face were covered by a dismal shadow. During a break in the seminar, I found a chance to talk to him. I asked him, "Is there something bothering you? Your face looks so sad and grey."

"No! Nothing is bothering me," he replied.

However, at the end of the seminar, he came to talk to me. He said, "I have not talked to my mom for six months." I asked him why. He said, "I had an argument with her over my girlfriend six months ago, and since then I have not talked to her."

"Why don't you call her and untie this knot?" I asked.

"I can't. I cannot surrender to her."

"Why not? Your mom would sacrifice anything for your happiness. She has taken care of you her whole life. Why can't you call her?"

He was silent and then left.

The next week at my final seminar, the young man returned. His facial expression was so different, bright and cheerful. I asked him, "Did you call your mom?"

"We will have dinner together tomorrow night."

Two Monks and a Lady
(和尚淑女)

One day many, many years ago in ancient China, there were two Buddhist monks walking on a country path. The day started out with the sun shining and the temperature mild, a nice day for walking, but early in the afternoon the clouds gathered and darkened, and in a flash, rain began to pour heavily from the skies.

The two monks sought shelter under the leaves of a big tree. When the rain stopped, they continued their journey on what was now a muddy path.

Soon, they came to a place where the road was flooded. It was impossible to walk through without getting their feet and clothes wet and muddy. There they saw a beautifully dressed lady on the other side of the puddle. She was crying. They asked the lady what was troubling her and she sobbed.

"I am on my way to see my mother. It is her birthday and these are my best clothes," she said, "but I cannot cross over to the other side without ruining my clothes."

One of the monks volunteered to help. He waded through the water, picked up the lady, and carried her to the other side. The lady thanked him profusely and continued her journey. The monks continued on theirs.

After a few miles, the monk who did not carry the lady spoke out in anger.

"Why did you do that?" he asked. "We are monks, and we are not supposed to touch women—especially such a young and beautiful lady. It is wrong for you to have carried her."

To this the other monk replied, "My brother, you are correct, but I dropped the woman off miles ago. Why are you still carrying her?"

A Blessing in Disguise
(塞翁失馬)

Often an event occurs that people think of as good luck, but the end results of which turn out to be disastrous. In the same way, an unlucky event can bring about happiness. Therefore, you should not lose your will to continue if an unlucky event happens, nor should you be too overjoyed or feel too self-satisfied because of a lucky event or because something you desire comes very easily to you.

A long time ago, there was an old man who lived on the plains outside of the Great Wall of China. The kind, gentle old man had only two passions in his life: his son, whom he loved more than anyone else, and collecting rare breeds of horses. Every day, the old man and his son would ride their horses together. Often they would travel great distances to trade horses. Their days were full; they met new people, discovered magnificent horses, and enjoyed the good fortune that life had bestowed upon them.

One morning, a servant accidentally left the stable door open and one of the old man's favorite stallions escaped. When the neighbors heard the news, they came to comfort the old man. They told him they were sorry he had had such bad luck. But strangely the gentle old man was not upset. He explained to his neighbors that losing the horse wasn't necessarily bad luck. There was no way to predict that the horse would escape. It just happened, and now there was nothing that could be done about it. He told the neighbors they shouldn't feel sad about what seemed to be misfortune.

One week later, the stallion returned home and brought with him a mare. This was not just any mare; it was a rare and valuable white mare. When his neighbors heard of the old man's good luck, they quickly came to congratulate him. But, again, the old man was not excited. He explained that it was not necessarily good luck that had brought him this new and beautiful white horse. It just happened, and there was no reason to get excited over it. A bit puzzled, the neighbors left as quickly as they had come.

A short time later, his son was riding the white mare, and she slipped and fell. She landed on the young man's leg and crippled him. Again, the neighbors came to the old man's house to express their sympathy for the bad luck that had befallen his son. One of the neighbors suggested that the old man sell the mare before she brought them any more bad luck. Others said that he should kill the mare for revenge. However, the old man did neither. He explained to the neighbors that they should not feel sorrow for his son or anger toward the mare. It was an accident that could not be predicted, and there was nothing he or they could do to change it. At this point, the neighbors thought the old man was crazy and decided to leave him alone.

Two years later, an enemy army invaded the country. To defend the country against the attack, all of the old man's neighbors' sons were drafted. However, because the old man's son was crippled, he did not have to join in the fighting. The war was very harsh and most of the young men in the village were killed, but his son was spared because he had been crippled by the white horse two years before.

Two Tigers

Once there were two tigers. One lived in the wild and one lived in a cage. Both tigers believed they lived in poor conditions. One day they decided to exchange positions. They were both very happy in the beginning. Eventually they both died. One died of hunger, and the other died of depression.

A Bowl of Example
(一碗之教)

Once upon a time in China, a father, a mother, their ten-year-old son, and his grandmother lived together in a humble home. Every meal-time they sat together around the family table. The grandmother was quite old. Her hands had begun to shake all the time, and she had difficulty holding things. Whenever she ate, her shaking caused her rice bowl to wobble, and she could not use her chopsticks properly. She spilled food all over the table at every meal.

The daughter-in-law was very upset by this. One day she complained to her husband.

"My dear husband, every time your mother eats she makes a mess all over the table. This makes me so sick I can't eat my own food!"

The husband didn't say anything. He knew he couldn't keep his mother's hands from shaking so he did nothing and hoped the problem would go away. But in a few days his wife spoke to him again.

"Are you going to do something about your mother or not? I cannot stand it anymore."

After arguing for a while, the husband sadly gave in to his wife's suggestion and agreed that his mother should sit at a separate table away from the rest of the family. When dinnertime came, the grandmother found herself sitting alone. And to make things worse, the daughter-in-law served the grandmother her meal in a cheap chipped bowl, complaining that the grandmother had broken so many good bowls.

The grandmother was very sad, but she knew she couldn't do anything about it. Alone, she began to think of the past and how much time and love she had given her son as he was growing up. She had always been there when he was sick or when he needed anything. She would feed him the choice bits of the meals and sacrifice for him with no complaints. Now she felt her family had deserted her. Her heart was broken.

Several days passed. The grandmother's smile began to disappear from her face. Her grandson had been watching everything. He went to her and said, "Grandma, I know you are very unhappy about how my parents treat you, but don't worry. I think I know how to make things right. I'll need your help, though."

"What do you want me to do?" she asked.

The boy smiled and said, "Tonight at dinnertime break your rice bowl, but make it look like an accident."

"But why?" she asked.

"Don't worry," he said. "Leave it to me."

Dinnertime came. She was concerned that her grandson's plan would make matters worse, but she decided to trust him and do as he had asked. When her son and daughter-in-law were not looking, she picked up the old and chipped rice bowl and dropped it on the floor, breaking it.

Immediately her daughter-in-law stood up, ready to complain. However, before she could say anything, the grandson stood up and asked, "Grandma, why did you break that bowl? I was planning to save it for my mother to use, when she gets old!"

The mother's face turned pale. She suddenly realized that everything she did was an example for her son. The way she was treating her mother-in-law was teaching her son how to treat her when she got old. She felt very ashamed.

From that day on, the whole family ate together around the same table.

A Bowl of Noodle Soup
(一碗湯麵)

Right before dinner, seventeen-year-old Xiaoying (小英) had another fight with her mom, and she rushed out of the house in anger. She hated that her mom kept reminding her to do this and do that and don't do this and don't do that. Xiaoying was so angry she forgot to take any money with her when she left home. All that was on her mind were her mom's repeated harangues.

She thought, "I am not a child anymore. Why does she still treat me as a child?"

She walked about an hour, and having left before dinner, she was getting hungry. She saw a noodle-soup stall on the side of the street and wandered back and forth in front of it, practically drooling at the delicious smells. The kind owner of the stall noticed her and asked, "Young miss, do you want a bowl of noodle soup?"

"Yes, but I don't have any money," she replied.

"There is no problem. Come in. I will cook one for you."

When the owner brought the soup to her, she started to cry.

"What's the matter, young miss? Are you OK?"

"I am so touched. I am only a stranger to you, but you treat me so nice. My own mother is so mean to me. I hate her very much. She always gives me trouble and treats me like a child."

"Young miss! How can you think so? I only cook one bowl of noodle soup for you, and you appreciate me so much. Have you thought of how many bowls of noodle soup your mom has cooked for you since you were born?"

When Xiaoying heard him say these things, it shook her.

"Why is it that a stranger offers me a little favor and I appreciate him so much? My mom has sacrificed her life for me and loved me and never asked anything from me. How could I fight with her about such small matters?"

Xiaoying thanked the man, got up, and ran to her home. Her mother was standing at the door looking tired and worried. Xiaoying realized her mom must have been outside waiting for her the whole time she was gone. Instead of yelling as Xiaoying expected, her mom looked happy to see her.

"Xiaoying, I was so worried. You were gone so long. You must be hungry. I have cooked the noodle soup you like."

Xiaoying hugged her mother and never wanted to let her go.

A Donkey, a Father, and a Son
(驢與父子)

A father and son were walking on a country road with a donkey. A couple passing saw them, and one of them asked in a loud whisper, "How stupid are they? They have a donkey but do not know how to ride it." When the father heard this, he put his son on the donkey and continued their journey.

Soon after this, a group of people passed. One of them said, "How disrespectful of this young man. He rides the donkey while his old father walks."

The father then asked the son to dismount, and he got on the donkey. Soon, another group of people passed by. This time, the father heard, "How stupid they are! Why don't they both ride the donkey? Instead, one is walking!"

The father then asked his son to get on the donkey with him. They continued on the road. Soon they passed a place where there were a few people sitting on chairs beside the road. They heard a lady say, "What a poor donkey. It is abusive that both of them are riding on it."

The father and son looked at each other and both got off the donkey. They picked him up and continued on their journey, carrying the animal.

Soon they passed another group of people. The people didn't say anything. They were laughing too hard.

The father and son both turned red with embarrassment. They put down the donkey and just ignored what people said on the rest of their journey.

A Farmer Buys His Shoes
(買鞋量腳)

Sometimes what is most obvious is not clear to us. If we remain open minded, however, we will see the different sides of a situation.

There once was a farmer who lived many miles from the city. All his life, he had never had extra money to buy a pair of shoes. Finally, after a particularly good harvest, he discovered he had enough money to buy himself a pair of shoes. He took a rope, cut off a piece as long as his foot, and placed it on the table.

After breakfast the next morning, he rushed into the city and went to a shoe store. When he got inside the store, he suddenly realized he had forgotten the piece of rope. He told the shoemaker what he had done and said he would have to go home and get the rope.

When the shoemaker heard this he asked, "Whose shoes are you buying?"

"Mine," the farmer replied.

The shoemaker then said, "But then why do you have to go home? Your feet are a more accurate measurement than a piece of rope!"

Do you know what the farmer answered? He said, "No! No! I'd rather trust my measurement than my feet."

A Fight of No Fight
(無爭之爭)

The best way to win a fight is without fighting. Often you can win a fight with wisdom, and this is better than physically beating someone up. Instead of aggression, use patience and endurance to succeed. Big successes always come from many little efforts.

Long ago there lived a farmer who owned a small farm. He had two sons. The elder son was named De-Xin (德信) and the younger son was named De-Yi (德義). He worked very hard to make the farm successful so he would be able to leave it to his two sons when he died. The farmer's wife had died when the boys were little, and the farmer was often busy. Without a wife to mother his boys, the farmer did not notice that his eldest son De-Xin often bullied his younger brother. The younger son, De-Yi, never complained to his hardworking father, and so life went on. The boys got older, and De-Xin took a wife. The farmer thought all was well.

One day, the father became very sick. He knew he would soon die. He gathered his sons together and said to them, "I wish to give this farm to both of you. Share it equally and help each other to make it successful. I hope it makes you as happy as it has made me." With these words the father quietly passed away.

The sons divided the land equally and set about building their own farms. Even though they had divided the land, they still cooperated, helping each other with the more difficult chores.

However, not long after the father died, De-Xin and his wife decided they had not received enough land. After all, De-Yi was single and didn't need as much land as they did. She began urging her husband to request more land from his brother.

De-Xin went to see De-Yi and demanded more land. Because De-Xin was much bigger and stronger, the only thing De-Yi could do was concede in angry silence.

However, De-Xin was still not satisfied. When he saw how easy it was to get more land from his brother, he demanded even more land. Again, De-Yi could only consent to his brother's demands. Still De-Xin and his wife were not satisfied. Finally, they demanded that De-Yi leave and give them all the land.

De-Yi requested help from his relatives and friends and begged them to mediate the conflict. None would help. They knew it was unfair for De-Yi to be forced off his land, but they were afraid because they knew De-Xin's violent temper.

Alone, De-Yi decided to take a stand for what he knew was right. He decided to stay, even though his brother wanted him to leave. For this defiance, De-Xin beat him very badly. De-Yi was forced to leave his home and become a traveling beggar.

One day, while traveling in the Jiu Lian Mountain (九連山) region of Fujian Province (福建省), he saw several Shaolin priests in town on an expedition to purchase food. He knew the Shaolin monks were good in gongfu, and he thought that if he could learn gongfu, he could beat De-Xin and regain the land that was rightfully his.

He decided to follow the monks to their temple and request that they take him as a student of gongfu. When they arrived, De-Yi asked to see the abbot.

De-Yi told the abbot his sad story and asked to be taught gongfu so he could regain his land.

The abbot looked at him and said nothing. De-Yi found the abbot's quiet stillness unsettling and calming at the same time. The abbot said nothing for what could have been either an eternity or a few minutes. De-Yi could not say. At last the abbot spoke.

"De-Yi. If you are willing to endure the hard training, then you are accepted as a student here." With deep appreciation, De-Yi bowed to the abbot.

Early the next morning, De-Yi was summoned to the backyard. The abbot was standing in front of a young willow tree, holding a calf. He said to De-Yi, "Before you learn any gongfu, you must first build up your strength. Every morning and every evening, you must hold this calf and jump over this willow tree fifty times."

De-Yi replied, "Yes, master. This is a simple task, and I will do it every day."

Every morning and every evening, De-Yi held the calf and jumped over the willow tree, fifty times.

Days passed, weeks passed, months passed, and years passed. The calf grew into a cow and the small willow tree grew big, and still every morning and every evening De-Yi dutifully held the cow and jumped over the tree fifty times.

One day, he requested to see the abbot. He asked, "Dear master, every morning and every evening I have held the cow and jumped over the willow tree, fifty times. I have performed this task for three years. Do you think I am strong enough to train gongfu?"

The abbot looked at him and the cow, and smiled. "De-Yi," he said, "you have completed your gongfu training. Your strength is enough to regain your lost land. Take this cow home with you and use it to cultivate your land."

De-Yi was puzzled. "I have not learned any martial arts," he said. "What do I do if my brother comes to fight me again for my land?"

The abbot laughed, "Do not worry, De-Yi. If your brother comes to fight you again, simply pick up the cow and run toward him. There will be no fight."

De-Yi bowed to the abbot, took the cow, and left the Shaolin Temple. Perhaps the abbot was joking with him, but the years of training had not only strengthened his body but also his spirit and patience. He accepted the abbot's wishes and returned home to cultivate his land.

One day soon after his return, De-Yi was on his way to the rice field with the cow when he saw his brother De-Xin running toward him, shouting in anger. De-Xin had heard about his younger brother's return and had decided to beat him and teach him an unforgettable lesson. He thought after this beating De-Yi would never again dare to return. De-Yi saw the malice in De-Xin's face and had a moment of panic, but he remembered the abbot's words. He picked up the cow and ran toward his brother.

De-Xin stopped. He just could not believe the strength his brother possessed. He turned around and ran away. He never bothered his brother again.

A New Lake for the Old
(新換舊池)

Wang, Anshi (王安石), prime minister of the Song dynasty (宋朝) was fond of public projects. An advisor named Liu, Gongfu (劉貢父), who wanted to gain the prime minister's good favor, offered a proposition.

"If you drain Liang Shan Bo Lake (梁山泊), you will gain eight hundred square miles of fertile land."

The prime minister was delighted and excited, but he asked, "Where will we put the water drained from the lake?"

Liu, Gongfu (劉貢父) said, "We will dig a hole the same size as Liang Shan Bo Lake right next to it to keep the water."

A Rich Man in Jail
(獄中富人)

Many people dream only of money. What do you think it means to be really happy and rich?

Once upon a time there was a man who worked very hard. Day and night he worked, and he became richer and richer. As the days went by and his pile of money grew, he began to worry more and more. He worried about how to make more money, but mostly he worried about how to keep both friends and enemies away so he could have his money all to himself.

He decided to construct a fence around his house. It was a strong high fence with a few small windows so the man could spot any intruders. He also made the walls of his house thicker. He put strong locks on all of his doors and even put bars in all the windows. The man turned his house into a fortress. He finally felt safe. He shunned all his friends and stayed locked alone in his fortress. All day long he counted his money and considered himself the richest and happiest man in the whole world.

One day a stranger was passing by, and he stopped and looked in the window of the fence. He saw the man sitting behind barred windows and counting his big pile of money with a big smile on his face. The stranger said, "Hey mister! Why are you so happy? You're in jail!"

The Man Only Saw Gold
(攫金之人)

There was a man in the state of Qi (齊) who desperately desired to have gold. One morning, he dressed himself with nice clothes and went to market. When he came to the gold dealer's shop, he seized a piece of gold and left without paying for it.

A police officer soon caught him asked, "Why did you steal the gold right in front of so many people?"

"Well, when I saw the gold, I saw no one—I saw nothing but the gold."

An Attorney's Only Son
(律師獨子)

Forgiveness is one of the greatest gifts one can offer to another.

There once was a man whose father was a famous attorney and a professor of international law. Many of this attorney's clients were big companies, and his income was extraordinarily handsome. But the lawyer also spent many hours in court defending people who could not pay him. And once a week he went to the juvenile prison and spent time educating the young prisoners.

This young man was the lawyer's only son. The lawyer focused his mind and efforts on making his son happy. He sent him to the best high school and college. They had a big luxurious house with a library full of books. They often traveled together to different countries. Most of all he was a kind and loving father. The young man considered himself to be the luckiest person in this world.

One day, the father and son were walking in a park, enjoying each other's company and talking about life. The discussion came around to the death penalty. The father said he was absolutely against the death penalty. He said many death penalty prisoners actually changed and became good people during their prison term. However, they had to be executed simply because they made a mistake once before. He said forgiveness is more important than punishment.

The man said, "Father, when you were a judge, did you ever give the death penalty to any prisoner?"

"I did," the father said. "A man came to my court charged with murder. It was revealed in the trial that he was known for his bad temper, and one day when he was working on a job, he had an argument with his boss and, in anger, he killed his boss. I was the lead judge on the case, and I sentenced him to the death penalty. When he was in prison, he repented. News came to me about how he helped establish better conditions for his fellow prisoners and the many projects he worked on to improve the prison. From all signs, he had changed into a good person. I tried and failed to acquire special amnesty for him.

"While he was in prison his wife gave birth to his son. When I went to see him to tell him I failed, he showed me the baby's photo. He told me that his young wife would probably remarry, and he was worried about the fate of his child.

"Right after his execution, I received a letter from him." The father took out his wallet and pulled out a faded letter. "I have kept this letter with me for the past eighteen years." He handed the letter to his son.

The letter said, "Your honor, I know you tried very hard to seek amnesty for me. Do not feel bad that you failed. I killed a man and I must pay. Karma, yes? I appreciate you forever. I have a last request. I know it is an unreasonable request. But, you are a good man, and I pray you will agree to do this for me. Please look after my boy and help him to avoid making the same mistakes I made. Please educate and guide him to become a good man."

After the son read the letter, he asked, "Dad! How did you look after the boy?"

"My wife and I adopted the child."

The young man was shocked and angry to discover the person in front of him was not his father but was instead the man who condemned his real father to death. After taking a few deep breaths as his father had taught him to do, he calmed down and realized the man before him was not a demon. This man had poured his love and care into him. "Even my real father had forgiven him," he thought. He was filled with a great sadness for the father he had lost but was also filled with a great happiness for the father he had found.

"Dad, let us go home. Mom is waiting for us."

"Thank you, my son," he said. "I did not expect that you would be able to forgive me so quickly."

The young man's eyes were filled with tears, but his words were clear: "Dad! I am your son. Thank you for loving me these past eighteen years."

An Untrustworthy Wolf
(狼心難測)

We should always show our compassion to others, but we should also be on high alert and aware that our compassion may be abused.

A long time ago, there was a scholar named Dongguo (東郭). Dongguo was known to have great compassion for all living things.

One day, he was riding on a donkey along the way to Zhong Mountain (中山) when a wolf came running up to him in great fright.

"Kind master!" the wolf said. "Please save me. I am being chased by wicked hunters. Hide me in your bag, and I will remember your kindness forever."

Dongguo was overwhelmed with compassion for the poor creature so he emptied his bag of the books he was carrying. He put the wolf inside the bag and packed the books around him.

A few minutes later, the hunters arrived and asked Dongguo if he had seen a wolf pass. Not wanting to lie, Dongguo merely said he had not seen the wolf pass. The hunters left.

Dongguo released the wolf when the hunters were out of sight.

"I am grateful to you for saving my life," the wolf said, without appreciation. "But after all that running to escape the hunters, I am so hungry and will die if I don't find something to eat. You should let me eat you if you want to save me."

The wolf revealed his vicious teeth with a snarl, catching Dongguo by surprise. It was Dongguo's turn to run to escape. He saw an old man approaching and Dongguo ran to him for help.

"What is the problem, young man?" the old man asked.

"When this wolf was hunted by hunters, he begged me to save him. I saved his life, and now he wants to eat me," Dongguo replied.

The wolf defended himself. "When he hid me away, he bound my feet, pushed me into the bag, and crushed me with his pile of books. I had to curl up as tight as I could, and I could not breathe. I heard him tell the hunters he intended to suffocate me in the bag. Tell me, why shouldn't I eat him?"

The old man looked at the wolf with concern on his face and said, "Show me what happened so I can see how you suffered."

The wolf complied and crawled into the bag. The old man immediately tightened up the bag and whispered to Dongguo, "Do you have a dagger or knife?"

Dongguo took a dagger out from his belt. The old man signaled for him to kill the wolf.

"Will it hurt him?" Dongguo said.

The old man laughed, "This is a most ungrateful beast, and yet you still have compassion. That is an admirable trait, but you are also very foolish!"

The old man helped Dongguo kill the wolf.

Arrogance Will Be Defeated
(驕兵必敗)

When you reach a position of success, it is important to remain humble, aware, and alert. If you do not, your self will defeat you. My White Crane master always said, "The taller the bamboo grows, the lower it bows."

During the Chinese Spring and Autumn period (春秋) (770–476 BCE), the lord of Qi, Huan Gong (齊桓公), led his troops to attack Lord Lu (魯) and succeeded in taking over many of his cities. Lu's friend, Wei (魏), came to his aid but was also defeated. Finally, Lu and Wei requested help from Jin (晉), another friend of the kingdom, and together they hoped to save their doomed kingdoms.

Jin's troops were large in number and highly motivated to save their kingdom. They gathered together with the troops of Lu and Wei to prepare for the battle the next day. However, Qi attacked that night. Caught by surprise, the united armies were defeated very soundly.

The lord of Qi reveled in this triumph and believed no army could defeat his powerful troops. The following morning, he challenged the coalition troops of Lu, Wei, and Jin to another battle.

The united troops of Lu, Wei, and Jin, quickly reorganized. The troops elevated their spirits to high levels of awareness and alertness and prepared to fight. They were well trained and disciplined, and they were fighting for their lives and their kingdoms.

The lord of Qi, puffed with victory, did not take this new battle seriously. He bragged that he would defeat his enemy in just a couple of hours, and he wanted to attack immediately. His military adviser tried to stop him, recommending they reorganize the troops and prepare them for the new battle

"What are you afraid of? Fighting against these weak enemies, there is nothing to be worried about." Before the Qi troops were ready, he gave the order to attack.

Qi's troops were almost completely destroyed.

A Beacon Destroys a Country
(烽火滅國)

The Chinese have a saying: "It can take three years to earn trust, but it takes only one day to destroy it. Once it is destroyed, it will take at least seven years to regain trust."

Self-trust is the root of confidence. You must learn to build up your confidence and demonstrate it externally. Only then can you earn the trust and respect of others. The Chinese also say, "A man cannot be trusted who will not stand in society" (人無信不立).

When Emperor You of Zhou (周幽王) (781–771 BCE) attacked the kingdom of Bao (褒), he won a beautiful lady named Bao Si (褒姒). However, Bao Si never smiled. The emperor gave her precious pearls and jewels to wear and delicious things to eat, trying to make her smile. He tried a thousand things, but still Bao Si would not smile. The emperor was the monarch of the country, and yet he couldn't win a smile from the beautiful lady. It made him very unhappy.

At that time, the country of Zhou had platforms for signal beacons around the borders. If an enemy attacked the capital, the beacons were lit to signal the feudal lords that their emperor was in danger, and they would immediately send out their troops to help. The beacons were not to be lit unless the situation was critical. However, one evening the emperor gave the order to light the signal beacons. He thought the spectacle would please Bao Si. When the feudal lords saw the lit beacons, they thought the capital city was in great danger, so a vast and mighty army of soldiers soon came running.

When Bao Si saw all the troops rushing crazily about and saw that the officers and men were very nervous, she unconsciously let out a great laugh. Emperor You was thrilled. He smiled and smiled and completely forgot about the lords standing at the ready, awaiting orders. After a while the emperor said, "It's nothing. Everyone go home."

In order to win Bao Si's smile, Emperor You completely forgot the importance of the signal beacons and went so far as to light them several more times. The lords all knew that they had been made fools of and were furious.

Later, Emperor You dismissed his empress, Lady Shen (申后), in favor of his concubine Bao Si. Lady Shen's father was greatly angered and humiliated. He united with a foreign tribe called the Quan Rong (犬戎) to attack Emperor You. When Emperor You's situation got urgent, he ordered the signal beacons to be lit to summon the feudal lords to save him and the capital. Even as the invaders killed Emperor You, not one lord came to save him.

Beijing Doll Maker
(北京娃匠)

Often a secret can be only a few sentences. The Chinese have a saying: "Great Dao is no more than two or three sentences. Once spoken, though, it is worth only a halfpenny." Understand that the secret often takes a master a lifetime to figure out.

Once upon a time, there was a master doll maker in Beijing who made beautiful dolls from clay. He was so skillful and famous that he had many students who also made dolls and competed with his business. Strangely, however, customers could always tell which doll was made by the master and which one was made by his students. The students tried but could not figure out what the master did to create his distinctive difference. That meant the master had kept some secret of making the doll to himself.

One day, this master got very sick and was dying. He thought that he should not take the last secret of doll making to the grave with him. Thus, he summoned his most loyal student to his room.

"I am dying," the master said. "Before I die, I would like to pass the last secret of doll making to you. However, you should remember that if you keep the secret to yourself, you will enjoy glory and wealth your whole life. But if you reveal it to others, you will have so many competitors, you will be as poor as others. Now, make a doll in front of me."

"Yes, master." The student went to get some wet clay from the workshop and began to make a doll as perfect as he could. He made a lovely doll. The student had developed his craft to a high level, but it still looked like the doll of a student and not a master.

"Look! When people buy a doll, first they look at the facial expression," the master said. "This expression must be as natural as possible. Now, pay attention. This is my secret."

The master placed his right index finger under the chin of the wet doll the student had just made and lifted it up slightly. The tiny lift gave the doll's face a subtle but profound difference in expression.

Boiling a Pot of Water
(燒一壺水)

An ambitious young man struggled for many years to achieve his dream of having a successful business. He worked very hard but he failed. Filled with frustration, he went to visit a wise man to ask for his advice.

The old wise man listened as the young man went on and on about all the things he was doing to achieve success. When the young man had exhausted himself with his own story, the wise man asked the young man to boil some water for tea.

"Yes, sir." The young man replied. He filled the large pot to the top with water and then went out into the woods in search of dried branches for the fire. However, before the water came to a boil, he ran out of branches.

So, he went back into the woods and collected more dried branches. This time he collected more than before. By the time he returned, the fire was out and the water was already cold. He had to start from the beginning. Before the water came to a boil, the young man could see he would run out of branches again, so he rushed out to collect more wood. He returned just in time to keep the fire going, and finally the whole pot of water was boiling.

"The tea is very good," the old man said. "And I can see that you are a very hard worker. But perhaps you worked too hard for two cups of tea."

The young man didn't want to be rude, but he didn't understand, so he said nothing.

"What if you had filled the pot with less water?"

Suddenly, the young man's face was shining. The old man continued, "If you use only so much energy, time, and money to do all the things you like to do, you will end up with nothing being done. Why don't you remove some of the projects that you wish to accomplish? In this case, with your limited energy and time, you can accomplish something. It is the same as boiling this pot of water. If you don't have enough branches, you should boil less water."

The young man was enlightened by this conversation. He stopped some of his projects and focused on the most important one. In just a few years, he had a successful business.

The Chinese have a saying: "If ten fingers grab one thing, you will have it for sure. If ten fingers grab two things, you may have it. However, if ten fingers tried to grab ten things, you will lose everything."

Break the Cistern to Save a Friend
(砸缸救友)

When a crisis occurs, in addition to wisdom and a calm mind, you must also be brave enough to execute your decision.

There is a story about a famous minister, Si, Ma-Guang (司馬光), who lived during the Song dynasty (1019–1086 CE) (宋朝). When he was a child, he was playing with a few of his playmates in a garden where there was a giant cistern full of water. Next to the cistern was an old tree.

One of the children was very curious about what was in the giant cistern, so he climbed up the tree to see inside. The other children watched as adventure turned into mishap. They stood in horror as their friend slipped and fell into the cistern.

The children were frightened. They could hear their friend screaming for help and thrashing in the water, and they did not know what to do. A few of the children were so frightened they immediately ran away. Si, Ma-Guang, however, without hesitation picked up a big rock, threw it at the cistern, and broke it. The water flowed out, and the child inside was saved.

The Buddha Crosses the River
(佛祖過河)

Time is precious. Often we waste our hours on unimportant things.

The Buddha was traveling through the country preaching. One day, he came to a river so wide and deep he needed to hire a boat to cross it. Nearby, there was a master who heard that the famous

Buddha was waiting to cross the river. He came to see the Buddha and asked, "Are you the famous Buddha?"

The Buddha humbly replied, "Yes, sir. Is there anything I can do for you?"

"Well! You may be the great Buddha, but let me show you what I can do." The master demonstrated his skills.

"See? I can cross the river by walking on the water's surface without a boat," he said when he returned to shore. "Can you do it?" the master asked.

"How long have you practiced to achieve this skill of crossing the river without a boat?" the Buddha asked.

"Almost twenty-five years," the master replied.

"Wow! Very impressive! But I can just pay fifty copper coins to cross it by boat," the Buddha replied.

Buying a Good Horse
(買千里馬)

There was a lord who wanted an extraordinary horse. He was willing to pay thousands of pieces of gold for that special horse. He searched for three years but could not find one.

One day, a brash young man came to see the lord and said he would find a good horse for the lord. The lord was delighted.

Three months later the man returned with a horse's skull. He proudly presented it to the lord and said he spent five hundred pieces of gold for the skull.

The lord was enraged. "I want a live horse," he said, "not a dead one. Why did you spend five hundred pieces of gold for this skull?"

The man answered, "The people now know you are willing to pay five hundred pieces of gold for a good horse even though it is just the skull of a good horse. The people are now thinking if you are willing to pay a high price for the skeleton of a good horse imagine how much you would pay for an extraordinary live horse. You will soon acquire one of the best."

Within one year, the lord successfully bought three excellent horses.

Fishing with a Carrot

A rabbit went to a river and tried to catch fish. The first day, he caught nothing. He did it again the next day, nothing. The third day, before he threw the bait into the water, a big fish jumped out and yelled, "If you dare use carrot as bait again, I will smash you."

Carry Thorns to Request Forgiveness
(負荊請罪)

It is easy to make a mistake but hard to admit it. If you are able to face your mistake and correct it, then you are a real, humble person.

Righteousness is a way of life. Righteousness means that if there is something you should do, you don't hesitate to take care of it, and if there is something that you should not do, you don't get involved with it. Your wisdom mind should be the leader, not your emotional mind. If you can do this, then you will feel clear spiritually and avoid being plagued by feelings of guilt. If you can demonstrate this kind

of character, you will avoid evil influences and naturally earn the trust of others.

During the Warring States period (475–222 BCE) (戰國時代), the neighboring states of Zhao (趙) and Qin (秦) often fought against each other. In Zhao's court were two capable and talented officers, a military commander named Lian Bo (廉頗) and a civilian official named Lin, Xiang-Ru (藺相如). The state of Qin dared not launch a full-scale invasion against Zhao because of the skills of these two men.

Lin, Xiang-Ru's began his service in a position far lower than that of General Lian Bo. His intellect and good sense soon garnered recognition and promotion. When Lin, Xiang-Ru was assigned as an ambassador to Qin, he won a strategic diplomatic victory for Zhao. The Zhao king began to appoint him to higher, more important positions. Before long, his rank was higher than Lian Bo's. Lian Bo was very unhappy and unwilling to accept what he felt was a slight to his own position. He kept telling his subordinates that he would find an opportunity to humiliate Lin, Xiang-Ru.

When Lin, Xiang-Ru heard of this, he avoided meeting Lian Bo face to face. One day, some of Lin, Xiang-Ru's officers came to see him. "General Lian Bo belittles you," they said. "So far he has only talked about what he intends to do you, but you are already acting in fear. We feel very humiliated by your cowardice and would like to resign."

"Before I accept your resignations, allow me to ask you a question. If you were to compare General Lian Bo to the Qin's king, who would be more prestigious?"

"The king of Qin, of course. General Lian Bo cannot compare with the king of Qin!" they replied.

"And when I was an ambassador to Qin, did I not have the courage to denounce the king of Qin right to his face?"

Lin's officers lowered their eyes.

"I have no fear of General Lian Bo!" Lin, Xiang-Ru said. "The state of Qin dares not attack Zhao because of General Lian Bo and me. If the two of us are at odds with each other, Qin will take advantage of this opportunity to invade us. The interests of the country must come first, and I am not going to haggle with Lian Bo because of personal hostilities!"

When word reached Lian Bo of Lin's reaction, he felt extremely ashamed. He tore off his shirt, and with a birch rod tied to his back, he went to Lin, Xiang-Ru's home to request retribution for his own false dignity. Lin, Xiang-Ru modestly helped Lian Bo up from the ground and held his hands firmly. From that time on, Lian Bo and Lin, Xiang-Ru became close friends and served their country with the same heart.

Carving a Buddha
(童雕佛像)

Once upon a time, there was a young boy who was about twelve years old. His parents were killed during a war, and he was left an orphan. He decided to go to the Shaolin Temple and ask for shelter. With luck, he might be accepted to learn gongfu. Shaolin means "young woods," and the Shaolin Temple, located on the Song Mountain in Henan Province, China (中國河南省嵩山), was one of the more famous places where monks and priests of the Buddhist religion lived, studied, and prayed. Many of these monks were skilled in the martial arts, which they cultivated to maintain their health and to protect themselves from robbers and wild animals.

The young boy went to the temple and humbly asked to see the abbot. When he was led to see the abbot, the boy knelt down on the floor. "Honorable master," he said, "would you please accept me as your gongfu student? I will respect, obey, and serve you well, and I won't disappoint you."

The abbot looked at the boy and said nothing at first. Many boys came to the temple, and although he felt compassion for each of them, he could not take them all. The ways of the temple were not easy, and not all were suited to life as a Shaolin monk. The abbot decided to give the boy a test before he could accept him as a student.

"Boy," he said, "I would like to teach you gongfu, but I have to leave the temple for one year to preach. You may stay here, but would you do me a favor while I am gone?"

The boy was glad to have a chance to prove he could be a good student, and so he said, "Certainly, honorable master! What do you want me to do?"

The abbot led the boy out of the temple and pointed to a big tree.

"See that tree?" he said. "For many years, since before my time as a monk here, that tree has shared its spirit with us. It has shared its patient energy and provided shade for our meditations. But its time has come to change into a different shape, and I have not had the heart to chop it down. I have always felt the spirit of a Buddha in the tree. Would you chop it down for me and carve away the tree to release the Buddha?"

The boy replied, "Yes, master! When you return, I will have finished the Buddha for you."

The next morning the abbot departed, leaving the boy to live with the other monks. A few days later, the boy chopped down the tree. The boy wanted to carve a beautiful Buddha and make the abbot happy. He worked night and day, carving as carefully as he could.

A year later the abbot came back from his preaching. The boy was very anxious and excited. He showed the abbot his Buddha, which was five feet tall. He hoped to earn the abbot's trust, and he eagerly waited to be praised.

The abbot looked at the Buddha, and he knew the boy had sincerely done his best. This boy is special, he thought. He decided to give the boy a further test. He said, "Boy, it is well done. But it seems it is too big for me. It is not the size I was expecting. Since I have to leave the temple again to preach for another year, would you use this time to make this Buddha smaller?"

The boy was very disappointed and unhappy. He had thought that when the abbot saw the Buddha, he would be accepted as a student and he could start his gongfu training. However, in order to make the abbot happy, he said, "Yes, master. I will make it smaller."

Even though the boy had agreed, the abbot could see from the boy's face that this time he did not agree willingly from his heart. He knew this time the test would be a real one.

The next morning, the abbot left and the boy stayed with the monks to fulfill his promise. The boy started recarving the Buddha, trying to make it smaller, but he was disappointed and unhappy. He had to force himself to do the work. After six months had passed, he found he had carved an ugly, unhappy Buddha.

The boy was very depressed. He was so unhappy that he stopped working. Days passed days. Weeks passed weeks. The date of the abbot's return was getting closer. His chance of becoming a student of the abbot was getting slimmer and slimmer, and his unhappiness was growing deeper and deeper.

One morning, he said to himself, "If completing this Buddha is the only way I can learn gongfu, why don't I do my best work and enjoy it? I made a promise, and I will keep it."

That morning he regained his patience and his will. Day and night he worked. The more he worked, the happier he became and the more he enjoyed his work. Before the boy noticed it, the year was up, and he had almost completed his happy and refined Buddha.

When the abbot came back, the boy went to see him with his new Buddha. This carving was two feet tall and smiling. When the priest saw the Buddha, he was very happy. He knew the boy had accomplished one of the hardest challenges that a person can face: conquering himself.

He decided to give the boy one final test.

"Boy," he said, "you have done well. But it seems it is still too big for me. In a few days I have to leave the temple again for another year of preaching. During this time, could you make this Buddha even smaller?"

This time the boy showed no sign of being disappointed. Instead, he said, "No problem, master. I will make it smaller."

The abbot left again. Every minute the boy could find he spent at his task of releasing the spirit of the Buddha from the tree.

One year later, the abbot returned. The boy handed him a Buddha, two inches tall and intricately carved. The folds of the Buddha's robe looked so soft they invited the hand, and the compassion of the Buddha was imbued in the eyes. The abbot now believed this boy would be a successful martial artist, for gongfu just means energy (gong) and time (fu). Anything that needs a lot of time, energy, and patience to do well is gongfu.

The boy went on to become one of the best students in the Shaolin Temple.

Clay Image and Wooden Image
(泥人木偶)

A wise man must see the possible development of the future and not be blinded by temporary benefit and advantage.

When the Lord Mengchang (孟嘗君) of Qi (齊) was deciding whether or not to take the position offered by Qin (秦), more than a hundred of his followers advised him not to do it. They reasoned that Qi was a small and weak country while Qin was a big and strong one. However, the lord decided not to listen to them.

One of his advisers, Su Qin (蘇秦), came to see him and tried to persuade him to change his mind.

"I have heard all of the arguments from your followers. However, all they were lacking was a supernatural understanding. My intention for seeing you is to discuss this supernatural perspective instead of mundane human affairs."

Su Qin told him a story. "On my way here, while crossing the River Zi (淄), I saw a clay image and a wooden image arguing. 'You used to be a piece of clay on the west bank,' the wooden image said. 'You may be molded into the image of the goddess now, but when the rainy season comes in August and the river rises, you will surely be destroyed.'

"'I don't think so,' the clay image replied, 'For you see, I was once part of the west bank and when the rain comes, the image may be destroyed, but I will just return from where I came. You, however, are an image carved from peach wood from the east country. When the great rain comes and the river rises, you will be swept away. What will you do then?'"

Su Qin then said, "Qin is a strong kingdom and has strong passes on every side. If you entered it I am afraid that you will be swept away and never return."

The Lord Mengchang gave up his plan.

Clench the Fist Tightly
(握緊拳頭)

An old man told a young boy, "Clench your fist tightly. Then tell me what you feel."

The boy clenched his fist for a short time. "I am tired," the boy said.

"Try to clench it tighter," the old man said.

After a few minutes, he said, "I am more tired now and feel suffocated."

"Now loosen your fist and see how you feel."

The boy released his grip and said, "Now, I feel very relaxed."

"You see," the old man said, "when you are tired, the more you clench your fist, the more tired you are. If you release your grip, you will be relaxed and at ease. You must know when to relax and ease the pressure or you will keep going till you collapse."

Confucius Learns the Chinese Zither
(孔子學琴)

There is a story about Confucius learning to play the zither, a Chinese stringed instrument.

Confucius asked Shi, Xiang-Zi (師襄子), a renowned musician of the time, to teach him to play the zither.

Shi taught Confucius a piece of music, and Confucius studied and practiced this piece. After a period of time, Shi, Xiang-Zi listened to him play.

"You have learned this piece of music very well, Shi, Xiang-Zi said. "You are now ready to advance to another piece of music."

"But I have not yet mastered the skills of this music," Confucius replied.

Shi, Xiang-Zi left Confucius alone to practice.

On returning and listening to Confucius play the piece again, he said, "You have mastered the skills of this music; you may advance to another."

"But I have not yet grasped the feeling of the music," Confucius replied.

Shi, Xiang-Zi left again, and Confucius continued to practice this same piece.

When Shi returned, he asked Confucius to play the piece for him. Confucius played it with a deep feeling for the music.

"Now that you are able play the music with feeling, you may advance to another."

However, Confucius said, "I still don't know the composer's feeling."

Confucius continued his practice and searched the music for the composer's feeling. After a period of time, Confucius experienced an epiphany. It felt as if he stood on high ground and gazed far ahead.

When Shi, Xiang-Zi next returned, Confucius said, "Now I know who the composer of this music is. This person has a tall body, his heart is wide open, and he has a farsighted vision for our country. If this was not composed by King Wen (文王), who else would have been able to do so?"

Shi, Xiang-Zi stood up, saluted Confucius, and said, "The gentleman you are talking about is a sage. This music, passed from him to us, is called 'King Wen's Practice'" (文王操).

Cooking the Hounds Once the Hares Are Caught
(兔死狗烹)

The Chinese have a saying: "When the goal is achieved, it is wise to retire" (功成身退).

King Gou Jian (勾踐) of Yue (越), with the able assistance of his generals Fan Li (范蠡) and Wen Zhong (文種), not only recovered the territory occupied by the Kingdom of Wu (吳) but also advanced an attack against Wu. As a result, Wu suffered a crushing defeat and Wu's king, Fu Chai (495–473 BCE) (夫差), was surrounded by rows and rows of Yue troops.

King Fu Chai decided to deal with the Yue king by trying to set his aides against him. He wrote a letter to Fan Li and Wen Zhong, which said, "When the hare is dead, the hounds will be killed and eaten by their master. When you have eliminated King Gou Jian's enemies, he will eliminate you, his advisors. Take precaution. Leave the Kingdom of Wu intact so you may have a route for your retreat!"

When Fan Li finished reading the letter, he said nothing. But after Wen Zhong read it, he pounded on the table and cursed King Fu Chai.

"If one must be a stooge, one must consider whose stooge he will be!" he exclaimed.

They disregarded the Wu king's letter and fortified their invading troops.

It became clear to the Wu's king that the country would imminently come under the power of his enemy. Defeated, he drew his sword and killed himself.

When the Wu kingdom was destroyed, Fan Li resigned from his position and went to the north to enter into the pottery business. Fan Li used the organizational and tactical skills that had made him a good general and created a successful business. He earned a lot of money and became a very rich man. Today, people refer to him as Tao Zhu Gong (陶朱公).

After Fan Li had left the Kingdom of Yue, he often thought of the words written in the Wu king's letter and was quite concerned about the safety of his old friend, Wen Zhong. He wrote a letter to Wen Zhong urging him to give up the riches and honor of his official rank and become a free and happy man. He wrote, "When the birds have been shot, all the good bows will then be stored away. When the crafty hares have all been killed, the master will kill the hounds to eat."

It's a pity that Wen Zhong did not listen to Fan Li. Not long after Wen Zhong received this letter from his old friend, King Gou Jian visited Wen Zhong. When the king departed, he left behind the sword that King Fu Chai had used to commit suicide. Wen Zhong understood the significance of this gesture, and knew he did not have a choice. He killed himself with the same sword his enemy had used to end his own life.

Cover the Ears to Steal the Bell
(掩耳盜鈴)

There was once a thief who heard that there was a precious bell in Fan's family (范氏), so he went to steal it. However, he was afraid that if the bell made noise others would hear it and he would be caught. He came up with a plan. He covered his own ears, believing that if he could not hear the sound of the bell no one else would hear the sound.

Dawn Three and Dusk Four
(朝三暮四)

A monkey trainer in Song (宋) was very fond of monkeys and kept a great number of them. He was able to talk to them and understand them. In order to support so many monkeys, he fed them the food from his own family's stores.

The time soon came when there was not much food left at home, and he needed to decrease the monkeys' supply. However, he was afraid that the monkeys would be angry with him, so he decided to deceive them.

"If I give you three chestnuts each morning and four each evening, will it be enough?"

All the monkeys rose up and with a great clamor expressed their anger.

"How about if I give you four each morning and three each evening?"

The monkeys quieted down and satisfactorily agreed.

Are you the monkey or the man?

Different Paths
(不同終結)

There were two young friends who decided to leave their village and go to the city to make their fortune. They worked hard for thirty years and each friend successfully earned a good amount of money. They decided to return to their village to enjoy their earnings and the rest of their lives.

On the path returning home, they encountered a wizened old man carrying a gong. He told the two rich old men, "I am the angel of death. You each have only three weeks to live. I will come to your homes in three weeks, and you will hear the sound of this gong. It will signal the time of your death." The old man struck the gong, and as the sound disappeared, so did he.

The old friends looked at each other in shock. They had worked hard, lived wisely, and thought they had many years left to enjoy. They resumed their journey with steps heavy with sadness.

When they arrived at their village homes, one of the men got more and more depressed, worried, afraid, and sad. He could not eat and could not sleep. As the days passed, his body weakened and his mind darkened. He sat waiting for the last gong sound.

However, his friend was different. When he arrived home, he thought, "Since I have only three weeks to live, I may as well enjoy it fully and share my fortune with all the poor people in the village."

He spent his days visiting his old friends and finding ways to help the people of the village. He was so busy sharing his good fortune he almost forgot he had only three weeks to live.

As promised, three weeks from their fateful meeting, the death angel arrived at the first man's home. When the man heard the sound of the gong, he died immediately.

At the home of the second man, his friends and the many families whose lives he had changed for the better had gathered to celebrate his life with lion dancing, drums, and firecrackers. When the death angel arrived, he kept hitting the gong, but its sound was drowned out by the noise of the celebration. No one was able to hear the death angel's gong.

The second man lived many more years celebrating each day as if it were going to be his last.

Divine Fish in a Maple Tree
(楓樹神魚)

There once was a huge maple tree at Stone Pavilion Dam in Kuaiji (會稽). The center of the trunk was hollowed from rot. Whenever it rained, the hole in the trunk would fill up with water. One day, an eel merchant passed the tree with a load of eels. He saw the tree hollow filled with water. Just for fun, he put an eel in the water of this rotten tree.

Not too long after, a villager found the eel in the tree. Since eels are not produced from trees, he believed this eel was divine and considered it a holy fish. After word of this spread throughout the village, people came to worship the eel and even built a temple for it, which they named Temple of Father Eel. They believed that if you prayed at the shrine, you would acquire good fortune. If you offended the Father Eel, you would be punished with calamity.

A couple of months later, when the eel merchant passed the maple tree again, he saw how absurd all of this had become. He took the eel from the tree and made a broth of it.

Disguise of Two Myopics
(近視作偽)

Two prideful old men, instead of admitting their eyesight problem, both boasted of their keen vision. One day, they heard that a tablet was to be hung in the nearby temple. Both of them secretly found out what was to be written on the tablet.

When the day arrived, both went to the temple. One looked up and said, "What a good writing it is! Doesn't it say, 'Brightness and Righteousness?'"

The other old man asked, "Don't you see there is some smaller writing on the bottom about the writer and the dates of writing?"

A passerby asked what they were discussing. When he was told, he laughed loudly and said, "It says the hanging of the tablet has been postponed."

Confucius said, "If you know, you know. If you don't know, you don't know. This is wisdom." (知之為知之，不知為不知，是知也。)

Doomsday of Cuttlefish
(墨魚末日)

The cuttlefish has eight legs it uses to draw prey into its beak. It can also hide its beak under its belly. When there is danger, it will emit a jet of ink to screen itself. It also often does this when it meets a fishing boat. Fishermen will cast their net on the inky spot and capture the cuttlefish.

What do you think? If the cuttlefish did not emit its ink, the fishermen would have a hard time capturing it. Sometimes how we react to perceived danger can, in fact, make us more vulnerable.

The Dragon and the Local Snake
(強龍與蛇)

According to Chinese legend, dragons are the kings of, and in charge of, all the water in the world. One day a dragon came to a territory where there were beautiful mountains, lakes, and rivers. He decided to settle down in this beautiful place. However, there was a snake already living there. When he saw the dragon begin to occupy the territory, he came to see the dragon.

"Sir, this is my territory, my place, and my home. You cannot stay here," the snake said.

"Oh! Ya! I am the dragon and in charge of all water in the world. If I want to take over this place, you don't have a choice, do you?" the dragon said and laughed.

"Oh no! You cannot take over. This is my place," the snake argued.

The dragon got angry and began to chase the snake and tried to kill him. However, the snake knew the territory very well, because he had grown up there. He could always easily find places to hide himself from the dragon. Every time the dragon tried to attack the snake, the snake found a way to sneak behind the dragon to bite his tail. After being bitten countless times by the snake, the dragon finally gave up and said, "OK. You are the local snake; you can have your territory back." The dragon departed.

When a person knows the local area very well, the Chinese always say he is a "local snake." This is a compliment to acknowledge that he is the master of the territory.

Drawing a Snake with Legs
(畫蛇添足)

Sometimes good judgment can be misled by pride and excitement. A wise man knows when to stop.

Three good friends were eating dinner together. There was one last dumpling left in the pot, and all three of them reached for it at the same time. They laughed, and each one said that he had a tiny empty space in his stomach that the dumpling would just fill.

One of them made a proposal. "Why don't we have a drawing contest? Each one of us can draw a snake, and the one who finishes first will win the dumpling."

The others agreed, and so the contest began.

One of the friends completed his drawing quite quickly. He was so proud of himself, and he thought, "I can draw so fast, I bet I could add four legs to the snake and still win." So he drew legs on the snake.

He finished his drawing and put down his pen to show that he was through. A second later, one of the others put down his pen, but then picked up his chopsticks, took the dumpling, and popped it into his mouth.

"Hey, why did you do that? I finished first, so the dumpling should be mine!"

"No," said the other, wiping his mouth with his napkin. The contest was to see who could draw a snake fastest. You finished first, but what you drew has legs, so it isn't a snake."

Dream of Cooking the Goose
(烹雁美夢)

Timing is often the crucial key to success.

One day a man was out hunting with his younger brother. When the older brother saw a wild goose flying over the sky, he got his arrow ready to shoot it down. He said, "If I bring it down, we will stew it."

His younger brother said, "No! I think it is better if we roast it."

They argued and argued. Finally, they found an old man to settle the matter. The old man suggested they stew half the goose and roast the other half. They agreed. They went out to shoot the goose. It was gone.

Becoming Rich with an Egg
(拾蛋致富)

Sometimes we fantasize about having good luck. If this remains only a fantasy, it will be just like a dream that comes and goes.

One day, a man, while walking on a country road, found a duck egg. He was so happy and believed it was one of the luckiest days of his life. He began to dream of how to take care of this egg.

"I can ask my neighbor, the old widow lady, to help me hatch this egg," he told himself. "She has a lot of chickens, and I believe she will not mind.

"After the duck is hatched, I can raise it and then sell it and buy more ducklings. When the ducklings grow up, I can sell them and buy more ducklings. Pretty soon, I will have a duck farm for myself and become rich."

He kept thinking about this good idea and was very happy. Lost in thoughts of his future wealth, he stumbled over a branch and fell down. The egg dropped to the ground and shattered.

False Dignity Gets Its Reward
(偽尊下場)

Many times we are fooled by our desires, which come from a false sense of dignity. For example, we may tend to show off our wealth to friends. However, someone who is truly wise is content with his talents and his possessions. He lives in humility and kindness.

In the Han dynasty (漢朝) about two thousand years ago in China, there was an old farmer named Chen Yin (陳音). For many years, he and his son worked very hard on their few acres of land and had gradually amassed a modest wealth. However, old Chen Yin was not happy. The one thing he regretted in his life was that he had never had any friends in the higher levels of society.

One afternoon, after a severe thunderstorm, Chen's daughter-in-law was washing vegetables by the riverbank. It began to rain again so she hurried home, and on her way back she saw a small boat anchored beside a willow tree not too far away. In the boat was a scholar who wore a handsome gown, which was soaking wet. The scholar's two servants were also soaking wet.

She greeted the boatman, who was an old friend of the family, and he introduced her to the passenger. The scholar's name was named Chen Yin—the same as her father-in-law—and he held a very high rank in the government. When she went home, she told her father-in-law about the coincidence of this high-ranking, elegantly dressed official having the same name as he did.

Old Mr. Chen picked up an umbrella and hurried to the boat. He said to the scholar, "What a storm! Would you care to take refuge in my poor house, honorable sir?" Feeling cold and hungry, the scholar happily accepted.

Inside, a nice, warm pot of tea was already prepared. When the scholar learned that he and his host had the same name, he was delighted. They drank wine and traced back their family trees as if they were indeed an old, happy family.

Old Chen gave orders for a banquet to be prepared. Then he took the scholar's hand and led him onto the porch, remarking, "I can't complain about the way things have gone in this village. We now own many acres of land. From them, I harvest ginger, taro, and sugarcane every year. There are also many fishponds, mulberry fields, and vegetable gardens. And many kinds of precious herbs are grown in the shade next to the mulberry fields."

Old Mr. Chen took the scholar to the other side of the house to show off some more, hoping to impress the high-ranking officer. He showed him ten tall buildings.

"Those are my granaries," he said, "and those are stalls for the oxen, the sheep, and the hogs. On the left you can see the houses where the tenant farmers live, and also the cottages we rent."

The scholar smiled graciously, his mind dazzled and his eyes greedy.

Dinner was announced, and the best wine and delicacies were served. Old Mr. Chen raised his cup and said, "This brew has been aged more than ten years. We offer it today especially for my honored younger brother."

The young scholar returned his thanks, and soon both were filled with warmth and spirit.

In order to impress the old man, the young scholar now started to brag about his connections in the government.

"Such and such, a governor, is my father's classmate," he said. "A certain first-rank officer is my uncle, and so and so in high government office is my best friend. Actually, I know almost all of the high-ranking officers in this province, and they would grant me any wish I made. In fact, anyone associated with me would be immune to misfortune of any kind."

Old Mr. Chen took it all in with enthusiasm and respect. When the meal was over, the rain had also stopped. It was getting dark, and the scholar had to leave for home even though old Mr. Chen begged him to stay for the night. Sadly, old Mr. Chen watched the scholar depart.

Next morning, old Mr. Chen put on his best clothes, gathered the best gifts he could find, and set sail with a few of his servants. When he arrived at the city, he called on the scholar, who received him cordially. From then on, their friendship deepened. For several years, old Mr. Chen sent the young scholar fresh produce from the farm, as well as preserved meats. However, the grateful scholar was pained that he could not do something useful in return for all the food.

Finally, he came up with an idea. He consulted a good friend, who was a police constable. The policeman arranged for a certain bandit to commit a crime and frame old Mr. Chen for it. Soon, the old man was arrested and put in jail.

Seeking help, old Mr. Chen's son rushed to the home of the scholar.

"Your father has treated me so generously. I will try my very best to save him," the scholar said with tears in his eyes.

"But the crime your father was arrested for is not a minor one. Your father cannot be released simply because I request it. He is involved with a bunch of real bad crooks. Actually, I do have an idea of how I should start," the scholar continued.

"I will spend as much money as I have to, as long as my father is set free," the son said.

The scholar told him how much he would need to bribe the magistrate's clerk, how much for the constable, and so on.

"Bribing these officers from the top to the bottom will take at least ten thousand ounces of silver."

In order to raise the cash, the son sold all their land. He had to give the deeds for the land to the scholar, who took possession of the property in the name of other officers. He also sold all of their possessions and within a year was reduced to absolute poverty.

While in jail, old Mr. Chen felt very grateful for what the scholar was doing on his behalf. Finally, he was released. When he returned home, however, he found that all he had left was his sorrow and his unhappy family.

After a few days, old Mr. Chen calmed down and started to wonder why a bandit he had never met could have wreaked such vengeance upon him. He cooked a chicken and prepared some wine, and took it to the jail. He hoped that the bandit would be grateful for the good meal and tell him why he had caused him so much trouble.

"I have destroyed you and your family, yet you still treat me kindly and come to feed me," the bandit said. "I cannot hide the truth anymore. What has happened was plotted by your brother the scholar. It is he who instructed the constables to arrange the whole thing."

Finally, old Mr. Chen started to realize what had actually happened. He went to the scholar's home but was told he was away on a business trip and would not be back for a long, long time.

Unable to see the scholar and vent his anger, old Mr. Chen went home and blamed everything on his daughter-in-law.

"If it weren't for you, the whole thing would never have happened," he said to her.

"I simply mentioned to you that you and the scholar had the same name," she replied. "I did not ask you to get involved with him."

In his anguish, old Mr. Chen cursed her. This caused her such pain she went and hanged herself. Her husband, heartbroken at seeing his wife dead for no reason, also hanged himself. Now, poor old Mr. Chen, alone and without any family or property, put a rope around his own neck too.

Foolish Old Man Moves the Mountain
(愚公移山)

One of the crucial keys to success is persistence. When you have a strong will, confidence, and persistence, you surely will be successful.

Taihang (太行) and Wangwu (王屋) were two big mountains a few hundred miles wide and a few thousand feet high. On the north side of these mountains lived a ninety-year-old man, called the Fool by his neighbors. His house faced these two mountains, and he found it very difficult and inconvenient to climb over the mountain to get to the other side. One day, he gathered the whole family to talk about this matter.

"If we work together to level the mountains, we can open the road to the south of Jizhou (冀州) and reach the bank of the Hanyin River" (漢陰).

All the family agreed, but his wife had a question.

"You don't even have the strength to level a small hill. How can you move two big mountains? Furthermore, where will you dump all the soil and rocks?"

He said, "We will move them to the end of the Bo Sea (渤海), north of Yintu" (隱土).

Then, the Fool directed his sons and grandsons to break the rocks and dig the dirt. Next, they moved the rock and dirt to the backside of the Bo Sea. A widow named Jing (京) with her eight-year-old son also came to help. It took a few months to make one trip.

A man called the Wise Man living near the river laughed at their efforts and tried to persuade them to stop. He said, "How stupid is this! It is enough to be a fool. You are old and weak. You will not even move a tiny fraction of the mountains. And you have to move such a huge amount of soil and rock to the Bo Sea. It is such a long distance away."

The Fool replied with a long sigh, "How shortsighted are you? You do not even have as much good sense as the widow and her son. Yes, I will die soon. But behind me there are my sons and my grandsons, their children, and so on from generation to generation. Since the mountains cannot grow bigger, why shouldn't we be able to level them?"

The Wise Man had no answer to the question.

One Perfect Kick

One day a student was watching her master practice. She watched in amazement as he executed one hundred perfect kicks. Each one was a picture of precision and power. When he finished she went up to him. "Master," she asked, "how did you do one hundred perfect kicks?"

"I did not do one hundred perfect kicks," the master replied. "I did one perfect kick—one hundred times."

Good Retribution of a Kind Heart
(好心好報)

It's easy to talk about righteousness. Living it is difficult.

This story happened in Jiangsu Province (江蘇省) during the Chinese Qing Guangxu period (清光緒) (1875–1908 CE). Mr. Jia (賈先生) was working for a big company and had earned a deep trust from his boss. One day his boss asked him to go to the southern side of the city to collect debts. Mr. Jia took his bag and left to do as he had been asked. After a whole morning of traveling and collecting debts from more than ten companies, his bag was full of silver coins, and he was tired and thirsty. He decided to stop by a teahouse to take some nourishment. After he finished, he returned to the office.

When he arrived back at the office, he discovered that the bag containing the money was missing. It was a lot of money, and he would never be able to pay it back. Even worse, his boss would never trust him again. He would lose his job and his good reputation. He was so upset, it took him a while to summon the courage to tell his boss. After telling his story, his boss prepared to take him to the police station. Mr. Jia thought his life was ruined.

Meanwhile, back at the teahouse, a businessman, Mr. Yi (義先生), had just arrived. Mr. Yi had just lost all of his money on investments that weren't successful. He had purchased a boat ticket and was resigned to returning to his home village. With a couple hours left before the boat took off, Mr. Yi went to the same teahouse where Mr. Jia had lost his bag, and he happened to sit down in the same place. When he sat down, he noticed Mr. Jia's bag. He sat in the teahouse for an hour, and nobody came for this bag. No longer able to stifle his curiosity, Mr. Yi opened the bag and was shocked to see a wealth of silver coins. This money could change his life, he thought. He could reinvest it in his business, and it would provide him with a luxurious lifestyle for the rest of his life.

However, Mr. Yi did not want to benefit from someone else's loss. He felt compassion for whoever it must be. He knew the person must be desperate and worried at such a loss. He waited at the tea house, sure that someone would return to retrieve the bag. A few more hours passed. His boat was ready to depart, but still no one came to claim the bag.

It was almost dinnertime when at last he saw a young man with the pale expression of someone in deep distress. The man entered the teahouse followed closely by two other people. This young man pointed at the chair, and Mr. Yi heard him tell the two people, "That is the chair where I was sitting. The bag could be there."

"Pardon me, did you lose this bag?" Mr. Yi asked "I have been waiting for you since this morning." He took out the bag and gave it to Mr. Jia.

Mr. Jia was so relieved that his body began trembling. He could not believe that he was able to find the money again. He looked at Mr. Yi with tears, "You are my great benefactor. Without this bag, I would have to hang myself tonight."

Earlier in the day, when Mr. Jia told his boss he lost the bag he pleaded for a chance to trace back the path he was walking in the morning. His boss did not trust him anymore and thought Mr. Jia would try to escape but he decided to allow Mr. Jia to look for the bag. To make sure he didn't run away, he ordered two other employees to follow him. They did not expect to find it.

After they introduced themselves to each other, Mr. Jia wanted to offer Mr. Yi a reward, but Mr. Yi politely refused. When Mr. Jia offered again, Mr. Yi again refused. When Mr. Jia tried a third time, Mr. Yi got upset.

"I returned this bag to you and was not expecting a reward."

Finally, Mr. Jia begged. "There are no more boats leaving tonight. At least allow me to treat you to a nice lunch tomorrow. I will wait for you in the restaurant next to the river. Please accept my invitation; otherwise, I will feel bad for the rest of my life." Then Mr. Jia left to bring the money back to his boss.

The next day Mr. Yi showed up at the restaurant where Mr. Jia was waiting anxiously. Before Mr. Jia could say anything, Mr. Yi bowed to him and thanked him. Mr. Jia was confused. He was the one who was supposed to thank Mr. Yi.

"Because of waiting for you yesterday, I missed my boat. When I returned to my hotel, I was told that the boat capsized and all twenty-three passengers were drowned. If I did not wait here, I would also be drowned. You have saved my life."

When Mr. Jia returned to his company, he told his boss what had happened. His boss was intrigued by the lucky fates of this chance encounter, and he insisted on meeting Mr. Yi. Mr. Jia's boss hired Mr. Yi as a manager of the company. Due to his reputation as a man of integrity, other companies trusted him and liked to do business with him. Soon, the company became one of the largest companies in the city.

Sharing Food in Heaven and Hell

A man died and was sent to hell. When he arrived, he saw there was an abundance of food on the table, but the spoons and forks had extremely long handles; they were longer than arms. All the people in hell were starving since they could not put the food into their mouths.

Later, an angel came and told him that they made a mistake. He belonged in heaven instead of hell. The angel brought the man to heaven. Upon his arrival, he saw the same scene: an abundance of food on the table and extremely long-handled spoons and forks. However, all the people in the heaven were happy and sated. They used the spoons and forks to feed one another.

Greediness Gets Its Reward
(假銀換真)

If you want a calm and peaceful life, you have to understand you get what you deserve. You shouldn't try to get things you haven't earned.

Once upon a time in the city of Qingzhou (青州), an old man came to a moneychanger's shop. "Excuse me, sir, but I would like to exchange these silver ingots for copper coins," the old man said. As the moneychanger weighed the silver, the old man chatted pleasantly with him about this and that. By the time the exchange was completed, the old man and the moneychanger felt like old friends, even though they had just met each other.

Just before the old man stepped out the door, a young man came in. When he saw the old man, he bowed to him with the greatest respect.

"Old Mr. Zhang (張), I did not expect to meet you here," the young man said. "I wonder if you still remember me. I do business with your son in Chongqing (重慶), and you and I have met briefly a few times in your house. I have just arrived in town to conduct some business, and was going to go to your home to give you some money from your son. Since you are here, I would like to give it to you now."

He handed the old man a package, bowed again, and left. The old man opened the package and found a letter and a large silver ingot. The old man turned to the moneychanger, who had listened to the conversation, and said, "I do not have my glasses with me. I wonder if you could read this letter for me."

Naturally, the moneychanger was glad to do so. In the letter, the old man's son discussed business conditions in Chongqing and asked his father to take good care of himself. At the end of the letter the son said, "Enclosed is ten ounces of fine silver. Please use this to help pay for your living expenses."

The old man said, "Since I am always using copper coins, why don't you also change this silver ingot for me. Actually, you don't have to weigh it again; according to the letter, it should weigh ten ounces."

However, the moneychanger decided to weigh the ingot anyway, just to be on the safe side.

The moneychanger was surprised to find that, instead of ten ounces of silver, there was actually 11.4 ounces. He assumed that the old man's son had made a mistake. He thought, "The old man cannot weigh this silver himself. Why don't I let the error stand and keep the difference?" And so he gave the old man nine thousand copper coins, which was the current rate of exchange for ten ounces of silver.

The old man took the coins, said goodbye, and left. A minute after the old man had left, a regular customer of the moneychanger came into the store and rushed up to the counter.

"That old man who was just here," he said, "did you do business with him? He's a con man, and for years he has cheated people with fake silver. He's probably cheated you too. I spotted him when he came in, but I was afraid to tell you this in front of him."

The moneychanger quickly cut open the ingot that the old man had received from his son and found that it was made of lead with only a thin coating of real silver. He was very upset. He thanked the man and asked him if he knew where the old man lived.

"He lives about a mile away," said the customer, "and there is still time to catch him before he arrives home. However, he's my neighbor, and if he finds out that I told you about him, he will find some nasty way to get back at me. If you give me three ounces of silver, though, I will help you find him. But please, don't let him know I told you."

The moneychanger had no choice but to agree, and so he said, "All right, just take me to him and you can leave."

He gave the man three ounces of silver, and together they left the shop and rushed to the east side of the city. Ten minutes later, they spotted the old man. He had stopped in a wine shop for a drink before going home. The customer pointed out the old man from a distance and said to the moneychanger, "There he is. Catch him quickly; I must go now." And he turned a corner and was gone.

The moneychanger rushed into the wine shop, grabbed the old man by the neck, and started to hit him.

"You dirty crook! How dare you cheat me! Did you think you could get away with giving me silver ingots with lead inside them? Give me the nine thousand copper coins back or I'll beat you to death!"

All this commotion soon attracted a large crowd of people, who restrained the moneychanger. The old man insisted to the crowd that he was innocent of any wrongdoing.

"I exchanged ten ounces of silver that my son sent me for copper coins in his shop. There was no lead hidden inside," he said to them. He turned to his accuser and said, "You claim that I used a fake silver ingot. Well, show it to me." The moneychanger took out the fake silver ingot, which he split in half and showed to the crowd. However, the old man said, "This is not the silver ingot I gave him. The one I gave him was real silver. Anyway, this ingot seems heavier than the ten ounces I gave him. Does anybody have a scale?"

They borrowed a scale from the owner of the wine shop and weighed the silver. Just as the old man had said, it weighed more than ten ounces; it weighed 11.4 ounces! This made the crowd angry, because they thought that the moneychanger was trying to cheat the old man, and so they beat him up and threw him out of the shop. The moneychanger couldn't say a thing in his defense, even though he knew that he was right. He left the wine shop bruised and burning with resentment.

Grind the Steel Rod into a Needle
(鐵杵成針)

The crucial key to success is not how smart you are but your level of self-discipline. Those who have discipline can accomplish any task they face.

Li Bai (李白), who lived during the Tang dynasty (唐朝), was one of the most famous poets in Chinese history. When he was small, he did not like to go to school; he often skipped classes and roamed around the streets.

One day, truant again, he went to play around in the city. He soon became bored with the city and decided to go out of the city and have some fun. It was sunny and warm, birds were singing, and all the trees and flowers were swaying, following the breeze. He was moved by the beauty of the day. He thought, "Such glorious weather. I am happy I didn't go to school."

He walked and walked and finally came to a small old cottage at the bottom of a hill. He saw an old lady with a head full of grey hair sitting in front of the cottage with a pestle in her hands and grinding it on a rock.

"Hey, old lady! What are you doing?" Li Bai asked.

The lady raised her head, looked at Li Bai, and smiled. "Oh! I want to grind this pestle until it becomes an embroidery needle." Then she bowed her head down again and continued her grinding.

"Embroidery needle? Is that a needle for sewing?" Li Bai asked.

"Yes, it is," replied the old lady.

"But this pestle is so thick. How long will you take to make it into a needle?" Li Bai asked.

"Even water drops are able to penetrate a stone. Why can't this pestle be ground into a needle?"

"But you are already very old. Can you do it?" Li Bai asked.

"As long as I have a strong will and patiently put my effort in it, there is nothing that cannot be done," the old lady replied.

After conversing with this old lady, Li Bai felt so ashamed that he could not stay in school and study patiently. After that day, he never skipped school again. When he grew up, he became one of the most famous poets in China.

Hard to Be a Good Person
(好人難做)

There was a small temple at the entrance of a village. In the temple, there was a wooden image of a deity. A man passing by found a ditch on his path. He took the wooden image from the temple and placed it on the ditch as a bridge.

Another person passing by saw the wooden image on the ground and felt sorry for it. So he restored the image to its original place. But the wooden image was angry because this man did not offer sacrifice to it. Thus, it placed a curse on him and caused the man to suffer serious headaches.

The spirits of the underworld were confused and asked, "Why did you let the one who trod on you go free, but punished the one who restored your position?"

The deity said, "You don't understand. It is easier to bully a good man than a bad man."

Hear and Talk on the Way
(道聽途說)

A student of Confucius was cooking rice soup for the group. He noticed there was some dirt in the soup. Immediately he scooped up the portion of the soup with the dirt and got ready to throw it away. On second thought, he believed he should not throw out this precious food. Therefore, he sucked the soup around the dirt and drank it himself.

By coincidence, Confucius entered the kitchen and saw his action.

"Why do you steal rice soup behind the backs of your brother monks?"

The student showed the dirt in the scoop and explained that he did not want to feed his fellow students dirt, but he did not think it was right to waste food so he ate the dirty portion himself. Chastened, Confucius realized he had made a mistake. He took a deep breath and sighed.

"Though I saw it with my own eyes, I still made a wrong judgment."

Help the Rice to Grow
(拔苗助長)

Many of our tasks must be accomplished slowly and gradually and require patience to finish. Sometimes you may think you have found a way to do something better or quicker, but actually you are just destroying it. A wise man learns from the past, proceeds carefully in the present, and thinks calmly about the future.

A long time ago in China there was a farmer who worked very hard in his rice field every day. Because he worked so hard, every year he and his wife had plenty to eat.

One day when he arrived at his field he noticed that some of the rice grew faster than the rest of the rice. Suddenly he had an idea. He said to himself, "How stupid I have been. Why don't I help all of the rice to grow taller? Boy, how clever I am to think of this!"

He went into the rice field and started pulling each rice plant an inch higher. He worked hard pulling the plants and by the end of the day, he had finished his whole field. He stood up and looked at the field, feeling smart and very proud of himself. He thought, "If I pull the rice up just one inch every day, then in only a couple of weeks it will be ready to harvest." He then went home to dinner feeling very satisfied with himself.

When the farmer woke up the next morning, he was so excited. He ate his breakfast quickly and rushed off to his field to help the rice to grow. But when he arrived at his field, he saw with horror that all the rice was dead. He realized that, as he pulled the rice to grow faster, he was actually destroying its roots.

Hou Yi Learns Archery
(后翼學射)

There is a famous story in China about a young man named Hou Yi (后翼), who decided he wanted to learn archery. He heard there was a famous archery master who lived in northern China, and he decided to ask the master to teach him. Hou Yi left his home in the south to search for the master in the distant northern territories of China.

After three months of traveling, Hou Yi found the home of the famous master. When he knocked on the door, the old master came out and asked, "What do you want, young man?"

Hou Yi kneeled down and said, "My name is Hou Yi. I have come very far to ask you to accept me as your student and teach me archery."

The master replied, "I cannot teach you. I am old and not as good as I used to be. Now go home."

But Hou Yi would not be discouraged so easily.

"Master," he said, "I humbly beg you to take me as your student. I have left my wife alone to care for our farm. I cannot leave until you take me as your student."

The master closed the door and left Hou Yi outside. Hou Yi was determined and remained kneeling in front of the master's house. Before long it got dark and started to snow. Hou Yi was very cold and hungry, but he did not move. One day passed, and then another. Finally, on the third day the master opened the door. The master said, "Hou Yi, if you really want to learn archery from me, you must first complete three tasks."

Hou Yi was very happy because now he would get to learn archery. "Yes, master," he replied. "What is the first task?"

"The first task is simple. Go home, and every night and every morning you must watch three incense sticks burn. Do this every day for three years, then come back to see me."

Hou Yi went home and watched an incense stick burn every night and every morning. At first, it was very boring, and he had to force himself to watch. He kept at it only because he wanted to learn archery so badly. After six months, watching the incense burn became a habit and he began to enjoy it. He found that when he enjoyed it, he was able to concentrate all his attention on the incense. When he did this, everything around him seemed to disappear, and the incense seemed to get larger and larger. He began to notice details about the incense that he had not noticed before, like how the smoke moved as it rose from the incense stick, and the subtleties of the smell of the smoke as it filled the room.

Without realizing it, he had learned a very important lesson that every good archer must know: how to calm down his mind and concentrate on one thing, and not to be distracted by anything else.

After three years, Hou Yi traveled to the north again to see the master. He was happy because he had finished the first task. He knocked on the door and the master came out.

"Have you finished the task?" asked the master.

"Yes, master," replied Hou Yi.

"And what did you see when you watched the incense?" the master asked.

"The incense became very big and clear to me, and I could see details that I had not noticed before."

"Good!" replied the master. "Now, for the second task. You must go home and watch your wife weave at her loom. Follow the shuttle with your eyes as it moves back and forth. When you have done this for three years, come back to see me again."

Hou Yi returned home, and each day he sat by his wife's loom and watched the shuttle move back and forth. In the beginning it was difficult. The shuttle moved very fast, and it was very hard to follow it with his eyes. It made his eyes ache to try to keep up with it. But after a year, he got used to the fast-moving shuttle, and his eyes did not bother him anymore. After two years, he found that he could concentrate on the shuttle, and it appeared to move slower and slower.

Without realizing it, Hou Yi had learned another very important lesson every good archer needs to know: how to concentrate on a moving object.

At the end of the third year, Hou Yi went back to see his master. The master said, "You have finished the second task. What did you see?"

"The shuttle moved very fast at first, and it was very difficult to keep my eyes on it," Hou Yi replied. "But then it started to move slower and slower until it seemed like it was barely moving at all."

"Good!" replied the master. "Now for the third and final task. Go home and make ten rattan rice baskets every day for the next three years, then come back to see me."

It is very hard to make Chinese rice baskets. You need to have very strong wrists and arms. A good basket maker has a hard time making five rice baskets in one day, and Hou Yi had to make ten a day.

Hou Yi returned home and started making rice baskets. At first, he barely got any sleep because it would take him almost all day and night to finish the ten baskets. His arms and shoulders were always sore and his hands were numb. But after six months his strength increased and he got used to the work. After a year, he could easily make ten baskets a day. By the end of the third year, he could make twenty baskets a day. He had completed the third task: he had developed strong and steady arms.

Hou Yi returned to his master's home in the north. The master said, "You have worked hard and completed all the tasks. I cannot teach you anymore." And with that his master turned and walked away.

Suddenly, Hou Yi realized that the three tasks he had completed were really the training that an archer has to go through. He had learned how to concentrate his mind, track a moving target, and had developed strong arms and a strong chest so that he could draw the bow and hold it steady. But he did not believe that the master had taught him all he could. Hou Yi decided to put the master to a test. By now, the master was a hundred yards away, so Hou Yi took an arrow and shot it at the master's hat.

The master heard Hou Yi's arrow. Quickly he turned and drew his own bow. To Hou Yi's amazement, the master's arrow struck his arrow in midair and both fell to the ground. Quickly, Hou Yi drew another arrow and shot it at the master. Hou Yi watched as the master drew and shot his second arrow. Again, they collided in midair.

Hou Yi saw that the master was out of arrows. He shot another arrow, thinking that this time he would hit the master's hat for sure. He watched as the master calmly broke a branch off a nearby willow tree. Using it as an arrow, he drew it back and shot it at Hou Yi's third arrow. Once again, he struck Hou Yi's arrow in midair, and both arrows fell to the ground.

Hou Yi ran to the master. He knelt before him and said, "Master, you have taught me one more thing. What I cannot learn from you is your experience."

The master replied, "Yes, that is the one thing I cannot teach you. You can only gain experience through practicing by yourself."

After many years of practice, Hou Yi became one of the greatest archers in Chinese history.

Learn What to Pick Up
(學會捨棄)

When you have an opportunity, do you know how to take full advantage of it? When it is no longer useful to you, can you let it go? The Chinese have a saying: "A wise man knows how to pick up and also how to drop it." (拿得起，放得下。)

Two friends went to a tall mountain to find precious stones. After a whole day of searching, one person had a full backpack of stones. However, the other person had only a few stones in his backpack.

"Why don't you pick up more stones?" the one with the full backpack asked. "There are so many."

"It is OK. All I want is the stones that are valuable and precious to me. I am satisfied with just a few."

The two friends started back down from the mountain. As they descended, the friend with the full backpack found the pack was getting too heavy and making travel difficult. Along the way, he kept throwing away the stones that were less precious to him. When they reached the bottom of the mountain, all he had left was a few very precious stones.

Learning Patience
(學習耐性)

The Chinese have a saying: "Knowing is easy and doing is difficult" (知易行難).

One day a man was about to leave to start a new job as a government official. His close good friend came to see him off. His friend said, "The most important thing for an official is to always be patient."

The man replied that he would. His friend repeated the same advice three more times, and each time the man nodded his head in agreement.

When his friend offered his advice the fourth time, the man became angry and asked, "Do you think I am an idiot? Why do you have to repeat this simple thing over and over?"

His friend looked at him with concern and said, "See! It is not easy to be patient."

The Final Goal of Practicing Archery
(練箭之的)

There are many ways to experience and understand the meaning of life. This is how the spirit grows. It does not matter what you are learning and perfecting; as long as you continue to try hard and have patience, you will soon reach a high level where few can match you. Through this self-conquering process, your spirit will grow. Once you have reached spiritual enlightenment, all of the skills you have mastered will become empty. My White Crane master always said, "Your self is the biggest enemy of you. If you can conquer your self, you will conquer any difficulty in front of you."

Yang, You-Ji (養由基), was a famous archer during the Chinese Spring and Autumn period (770–476 BCE). Because he was so famous, there are many legends about his skill. Here is one of them.

At a young age, Yang, You-Ji had already reached a high level of skill and was well known in the village. He was very proud of himself for his achievement. One day, he heard the sound of something hitting metal. Curious, he went out of the house to see from where the sound came. He saw an old man using a spoon to hit a copper bowl. He was selling cooking oil. When people heard the sound, they knew the oil seller was there.

Yang, You-Ji watched as the old man placed an oil jar on the ground. He then got a whole scoop of oil in his ladle. Without squatting down, the old man, poured the oil from his ladle in one slender stream into the jar. Not the slightest bit of oil touched the opening of the oil jar. Yang, You-Ji was amazed at the precision of this old man's skill. He knew that reaching such a level of accuracy was not easy. He said to the old man, "Hey, old man! How do you do it? It is extremely difficult what you did."

The old man looked up and immediately recognized Yang, You-Ji. "Do you want to see more?" he asked.

"Oh ya! Please," Yang replied.

The old man had Yang, You-Ji bring a bench from the house and set it down next to an oil jar. He then placed a coin over the opening of the jar. Ancient Chinese coins had a tiny hole in the center for threading purposes. Standing on the bench with his full ladle, the old man poured the oil smoothly into the jar through the coin's tiny hole. The oil did not even touch the edges of the hole. Yang, You-Ji was stunned at what this old man could do.

"How did you do it, old man?"

The old man smiled. "It is the same as your archery. When you practice more than others, you become better at it than the others. I have been selling oil for nearly forty years."

Yang, You-Ji was humbled and inspired by this simple seller of cooking oils. He returned to his practice with new purpose. By the time he reached his twenties, he had become one of the best archers in the country.

News of Yang, You-Ji's skills reached the emperor. Yang was summoned to court by the emperor, and he became the emperor's bodyguard. However, he was not happy living in the palace. After a few years, he left the palace and disappeared from society.

For more than forty years, Yang, You-Ji remained in seclusion. One day an old friend from the royal court decided to see if he could find Yang, You-Ji. After a few years of investigation, someone mentioned there was an old man in Tian Mountain (天山) of Xinjiang (新疆) who fit the description of Yang, You-Ji. His friend went there to check if that person was his old friend.

It took two months to reach Tian Mountain. After searching in the woods of Tian Mountain for many days, he came upon a simple cottage. An old man stepped out to greet him. They looked at each other for a while and slowly, seeing through the years, joyfully recognized each another.

Yang, You-Ji invited his old friend into his home. When they entered the cottage, the friend put the bow and arrows he carried with him on the table. When Yang, You-Ji saw them he asked, "What are these funny things you carry?"

His friend paused. At first he wondered if old age had clouded the mind of this famous archer. He took a long moment to ponder the situation, and finally it came to him. He said, "You must be the best archer in history. You have passed the stage of archery."

Lost Sheep in Many Paths
(歧路亡羊)

Often we are interested in many things, but our time is limited. If we spend all our time pursuing all the interests we have, we will not accomplish much. Everything we learn will remain shallow. Therefore, once you have chosen the one thing you are really interested in, you should stay on it and achieve the final goal you have set.

One of Yang Zi's (楊子) neighbors lost one of his sheep. In addition to sending all his men out to find it, he asked Yang Zi to send his servant to join them.

"Do you really need so many men to find a sheep?" he asked the neighbor.

"There are so many paths that the sheep may take," he explained.

Later, when Yang Zi's servant returned, he asked, "Well? Did you find the sheep?" .

"No, master! We did not find the sheep," the servant replied.

"Why couldn't you find a single sheep with so many men?" Yang Zi asked again.

"There are too many paths. One path leads to another, and soon we didn't know which one to take, so we returned," replied the servant.

On hearing this, Yang Zi became quiet, and the servant could see Yang Zi was deep in thought, so he left. Yang Zi kept silent for the whole day, never smiling. A student named Meng Sun Yang asked, "Losing a sheep is not a serious thing, especially if it's not even yours. Why do you lose your smile and keep silent for the whole day?"

Yang Zi did not reply. Meng Sun Yang (孟孫陽) met with Xin Du Zi (心都子) and described to him what had happened.

Xin Du Zi said, "When there are so many paths, a man cannot find his sheep. When a student has too many interests and distractions, he will waste his time. The origin of all knowledge remains one, but the paths of learning are many. Only if one is able to return to his primal truth can he avoid losing his way. You are Yang Zi's student, yet you have failed to understand him completely."

Mark the Boat to Find the Sword
(刻舟求劍)

A man of Chu (楚) was ferrying across a river. Distracted by the beauty of the river he carelessly dropped his sword into the water. Immediately, he made a mark on the side of the boat.

"This is where the sword dropped," he said to no one in particular.

When the boat stopped, he got into the water to find the sword, following the mark he had made on the boat.

Money Is More Important Than Life
(錢比命重)

Whenever it is necessary to get rid of something, do it without hesitation. Do not allow material objects to enslave you. Life is more important than anything in the world.

Yongzhou (永州) was built near a river, and so most of its residents learned to swim at an early age. One day the river overflowed and flooded the land. About a half dozen people needed to cross the turbulent river in a small boat. The boat capsized midstream, and they all started to swim. However, there was one who was swimming vigorously but making little progress. One of his companions asked, "You are a better swimmer than any one of us. Why are you struggling and behind?"

"I have one thousand coins tied around my waist," said the man.

"Why don't you throw them away?" urged his companions.

The man did not answer, but just shook his head "no" and continued to struggle across. The others reached the shore and shouted to him, "Throw away the coins. You are such a fool. What is the use of money if you drown?"

Still, he shook his head. Not too long afterward, he drowned.

The Mother of Mencius Breaks the Loom
(孟母斷杼)

When Mencius was a boy, he liked to play and didn't take serious interest in learning. One day, Mencius ran away from his class and went home. When his mother saw him, she picked up a pair of scissors and cut up the cloth she was weaving. Mencius was surprised and confused. He said, "Mom! It took you a long time to weave the cloth. Why did you cut it? Now, it is useless."

His mother looked at him and said, "Look, my son. Studying is just like weaving a piece of cloth. If you lose patience and interrupt it, like this cut-up cloth, it will be useless."

Mencius went back to school and never ran away from his studies again. Today he is known as one of the greatest philosophers in Chinese history.

The Mother of Mencius Moves Three Times
(孟母三遷)

As parents and teachers, we must show good examples to our children and students.

This is another story about Mencius and his mother. When Mencius was only three years old, his father passed away. His mother worked hard to raise him.

As a boy, he had a talent for imitating. At one time, his mother and he were living near a cemetery. Mencius began imitating the mourners, kneeling in front the tomb, crying, and worshipping the dead. When his mother saw this, she knew this place was not a good place to raise her son. She moved.

She settled down in a new place that was next to a butcher's factory. Soon, Mencius imitated the butchers. His mother realized that the new place was also not good for her son's growth. She moved again.

This time they moved next to a school. Soon, Mencius began imitating the students. He started to study, read books, and display good manners. They did not move again.

No Dregs for the Swine
(只是沒糟)

We often fail to appreciate what we have; instead, we focus on what we don't have. This kind of greedy attitude is the origin of depression and unhappiness. The Chinese have a saying: "Those who are satisfied are always happy" (知足常樂).

Thirty miles to the west of Hefu Mountain (河洑山), there was a small temple dedicated to a lady named Wang, Po (王婆). No one knew when or where it was that this lady lived, but there is a story about her.

It was said Wang, Po brewed wine and sold it for a living. There was a Daoist monk who often came to her shop and drank her wine but never paid. Wang, Po did not mind and always treated him nicely. One day, the monk told her, "I have never paid you for the wine I drank, and you still treated me kindly. To thank you, I will sink a well for you."

So the monk sank a well for the lady. "This is my payment for your kindness!" he said. Then he left. Wang, Po found that the well produced not water, but the best, most mellow wine the villagers had ever tasted.

Wang, Po no longer needed to brew wine. She just sold the wine from the well. Customers loved the wine and business increased rapidly; in just three years, she became very rich.

One day, the monk returned and the lady thanked him. "But," she said, "the well is very good in producing good wine, but there are no dregs for the swine."

When the monk heard this greedy demand, he laughed and wrote a poem on the wall:

High is the sky but not really high.
But human greediness is the one really high.
With well she sold the best wine.
Still she complains there are no dregs for her swine.

The monk left, and the well never again produced wine.

No More Space
(無地可容)

There once was a young man who was very interested in learning martial arts. He searched for nearly ten years, but he could not find a good teacher. One day, in a high remote mountain area, he heard the people of the village talking about an old master. From the reverence with which the people spoke of the master the boy knew that his search was over. He decided to seek out this master and ask him to teach him martial arts.

The master's home was deliberately not easy to find. But the young man persevered and finally found the mountain cottage. He knocked at the door and humbly asked to see the master. He was asked to wait in a little room and eventually the master appeared. The young man knelt down on the ground and bowed.

"Honorable master," he said, "I wish to learn martial arts from you. I have searched for ten years to find someone like you. Would you please take me as your student?"

This master did indeed have a high level of martial arts under-standing and skills, and he already had many students. It was diffi-cult to reject such a sincere young man, but he did not want to accept any more students. Without saying a word, the master went to the kitchen and brought back a teapot and teacup. He placed the teacup in front of the young man and poured the tea. He kept pouring till the tea reached the rim of the cup and there was no more space.

The young man understood that the master was implying there was no space for him. He was saddened and bowed his head. Head down, he saw a piece of straw on the ground. He picked it up and carefully inserted the piece of straw into the teacup, from the edge, without spilling any of the water out of the cup. He then looked up, hopefully, into the master's eyes. "See master, there is room for one more," the expression in his eyes said.

The master, impressed by this boy's perception and quick think-ing, accepted him as a student.

Nonsense of Flattering
(瞎扯奉承)

There were two men chatting in Shandong (山東). One was rich and the other was poor. The rich man asked the poor man, "If I give you twenty of my hundred gold pieces, will you flatter me?"

"But it will not be a fair share. Why should I flatter you?" the poor man answered.

"How about if I give you half? Will you flatter me?" the rich man asked again.

"In this case, we will be equal. Then there is no reason to flatter you," the poor man replied.

"Well! How about if I give you all of one hundred gold pieces? Will you flatter me?" the rich man asked again.

"It will be ridiculous. If I have all your gold, why would I need to flatter you?" the poor man replied with laughter.

Stubbornly Mistaken
(死不認輸)

Those who are wise and brave will recognize their mistakes and face them. The truth is always truth. That will not change.

There was a man in Chu (楚) who had never seen ginger and did not know how it grew. He thought it was grown on trees.

One day he met a man who told him that ginger was found in the ground. However, he would not believe it. He told the man, "I will make a bet with you. I'll wager my donkey. Let us ask ten people and see what they say. If all of them say that ginger is found in the ground, you may have my donkey."

They found ten men and all said ginger was found in the ground. Finally, he said, "Take the donkey. But it does not matter. I know ginger grows on trees."

One Bowl of Rice
(一碗白飯)

There once was a young scholar who was from a poor but aristocratic family. His family used most of their money to make sure he got an education, but he had limited funds to survive. He tried to spend his money frugally and not increase his parents' financial burden.

One day he went to a small shop for dinner.

"Sir," he said to the proprietor, "all I need is a bowl of rice for dinner, and one to take with me for my lunch tomorrow."

The shop owner could see from the student's clothing that he was poor and he was trying to save money by ordering the cheapest food.

He went to the kitchen and brought the student a bowl of rice. Underneath the rice he secretly hid an egg and some meat. He also put an egg and some vegetables in the rice the student wanted for the next day's lunch. As the student paid for his order, the owner said, "Enjoy your meal, young scholar, and please come back again tomorrow night if you like my food."

When the student ate his meal, he discovered the extra food hidden underneath the rice. After he finished the rice, he smiled to the owner and bowed.

At lunch the next day, he discovered that the owner had again included an extra treat underneath the rice. Tears of gratitude filled his eyes. He returned often to the same shop for his dinner and lunch and gratefully benefited from the secret treatment. The owner never mentioned this kindness.

Four years later, the scholar was given a good position in government and the owner did not see him again. One day twenty years later, the owner of the shop received a notice from the government that his business would be forced to relocate due to new road construction.

The shop owner was very depressed. This was unexpected, and he and his wife did not have enough money to move to a new area and open another shop. Furthermore, he would lose all his old customers if he moved away.

In the midst of their frustrating situation, a gentleman came to visit.

"The administrator of the town has asked me to invite you to open a shop near our building," he said. "We will supply all the cooking equipment and facilities you require. You will also be paid a regular salary, plus you keep any profit you make."

The man and his wife were stunned by this generous offer. They immediately accepted. They were puzzled about why they had been blessed with such good fortune but grateful and hopeful about their future.

Among the guests who came to celebrate the grand opening of his new shop was the scholar the owner had generously fed twenty years before. The scholar was the new town administrator.

Painting Ghosts Is Easiest
(畫鬼最易)

There was an artist who worked for the lord of Qi (齊). The lord asked, "What is the hardest object to paint?"

"Things such as dogs or horses are the hardest objects to paint," the artist answered.

"Then, what is the easiest thing to paint?" the lord asked again.

"Ghosts and monsters are easiest to paint."

"Why is that?" the lord asked.

"It is because everyone knows what the dogs and horses look like. That is why they are hardest to paint. However, nobody has ever seen ghosts or monsters so they are easy to paint."

Praying Mantis Seizes the Cicadas
(螳螂補蟬)

We often get excited about what we see in the future, ignoring the potential consequences. Life is just like playing chess. Every step can bring about many results. Are you walking in your life carefully?

During the Chinese Spring and Autumn period (春秋時代) (770–476 BCE), the king of Wu (吳王) was preparing to attack the neighboring country of Chu (楚). Many of his high-ranking officers opposed his ambition. The king of Wu became very angry and issued a challenge: "If there is anyone who dares to oppose my attack of Chu, I will put him to death."

Of course no one dared to speak out. One low-ranking officer knew the king was making a mistake but couldn't speak out for fear of being executed. He wanted to help his king so he came up with another way of conveying his message. Early one morning he took his sling shot and went out into the palace garden. He did this for several mornings even though the early morning dew soaked into his clothes. The king found out and one morning went out to talk with the officer. "Why do you stand in the garden each morning? You must be chilled; your clothes are soaked from the dew."

"Your Majesty! There is a cicada on the tree. It is happy singing and drinks the dew on the tree. It does not know there is a praying mantis behind it, ready to charge. While the praying mantis is ready to charge at his prey, it does not know there is an oriole hidden behind the branches, ready to peck the praying mantis. This oriole does not know I have already aimed at it with my slingshot and am ready to shoot my pellet. The only concern these three creatures have is the seeming benefit in front of them. They are not paying attention to the danger behind."

When the king heard this, he woke up and cancelled his plans to attack Chu.

Presenting Doves for the New Year
(新年獻鳩)

Often we just ask for what we want and do not ask where it came from. We do not think of the consequence.

It was a custom in Handan (邯鄲) for the people to catch doves to present to the lord, Jian Zi (簡子), for the Chinese New Year. The lord was very pleased at the people's sign of affection, and he gave a rich reward to the presenters. A close advisor asked the lord how this custom began. "Many years ago, I set doves free during the Chinese New

Year to show my kindness," the lord said. "Thereafter, the people began to present me with doves each new year."

"The people know you want doves so you can set them free so they all put their efforts in to catching them," the advisor said. "Unfortunately, the result is that many doves are killed in the process. If you really want to save doves and show your kindness, you should forbid people from catching them. The damage you have caused cannot be made up with your kindness."

The lord agreed.

Pretending to Be an Expert on Reed Pipes
(濫竽充數)

Confucius said, "If you know, you know. If you don't know, you know you don't know. This is wisdom." You may fool a group of people for a short time, but you cannot fool a single person for a long time.

The lord of Qi, Xuan (齊宣王), enjoyed reed pipe music. He particularly liked listening to a large group playing at the same time.

A scholar named Nanguo (南郭) requested a place in the orchestra. The lord liked this scholar and so without an audition he granted Nanguo a place in the orchestra with a salary that was enough to feed several hundred men.

After the Lord Xuan died, Lord Min (湣王) succeeded the throne. Lord Min liked the sound of a solo reed playing.

The scholar fled.

Qi Xi Requests Retirement
(祁奚請老)

There once was a high-ranking official named Qi Xi (祁奚), who lived in the state of Jin (晋) during the Chinese Spring and Autumn period (770–476 BCE) (春秋時代). When Qi Xi was old and ready to retire, Duke Dao of Jin (晋悼公) asked him to recommend a candidate to replace him. Qi Xi said, "Xie Hu (解狐) is an excellent man who is most suitable to replace me."

"Isn't Xie Hu your political enemy? Why would you recommend him?" Duke Dao asked.

"You only asked me who is suitable and most trustworthy for the job," Qi Xi replied. "You didn't ask me who was my enemy. I only recommended who I think is the best for this position."

Unfortunately, before Duke Dao could assign Xie Hu the new position, Xie Hu died of sickness. Duke Dao asked Qi Xi to recommend another person for his position.

Qi Xi said, "Now that Xie Hu is dead, the only person who can take my place is Qi Wu" (祁午).

"Isn't Qi Wu your son? Aren't you afraid that there may be gossip?"

"You asked me who was the most suitable for the position. You did not ask if Qi Wu was my son. I only replied with who was the best choice for my replacement."

As Qi Xi predicted, his son Qi Wu was an extremely capable and effective official. People had faith that a virtuous man like Qi Xi would recommend a really talented man. He would not withhold praise of an enemy, and he would not promote his own son out of selfishness.

Right or Wrong in Sinking a Well
(鑿井是非)

Once there was a well dug beside a well-traveled road. All who traveled this road benefited from the well. The well provided fresh water to satisfy their thirst during their journey. They all appreciated that this well was there.

One night, a careless person fell into the well and drowned. The people blamed the person who dug the well.

A Raven and a Rabbit

A raven landed on a high branch and rested. A rabbit saw him. He asked, "Can I be like you, doing nothing, just resting?"

"Of course you can."

The rabbit sat under the shade of the tree, resting and doing nothing. Suddenly a fox appeared, caught him by surprise, and ate him.

River Deity Gets Married
(河伯娶婦)

Throughout human history, people have been deceived, manipulated, and sacrificed for others' ambitions. Can we free ourselves of this physical and spiritual bondage imposed on us through the beliefs of others?

During the Chinese East Zhou period (770–221 BCE) (東周), Xi, Menbao (西門豹) was assigned to be governor of Ye City (鄴城) by the lord of Wei (魏文侯). When Xi arrived at the city, he summoned a few senior officials to his office and asked them why the people of the city seemed so depressed and why, for such a large city, only a few people lived there.

"It is because the river deity gets married every year," one of the officials replied.

"Please tell me more about this river deity's marriages," the governor said.

"As you know, Your Honor, the Zhang River (漳河) runs through this area. The god of this river is the river deity. This god loves young and beautiful women. He demands that we offer him a beautiful woman each year. This marriage assures he will protect the area and bring us a good harvest. If we do not offer him a bride, he will flood the area and make the people suffer," the senior official replied.

"How did this custom start?" the governor asked.

"It was begun by the sorceress. It is she who told us of the river deity's wishes. Since everyone is afraid of flooding, no one dares to go against her. The sorcerer has three acolytes, who each year visit the families of the county and select a beautiful young lady to be the river deity's bride. Rich families will pay a large amount of money as ransom to keep their daughters safe. The poor families have no choice but to sacrifice their daughters. The day before the marriage, the bride will cleanse her body. She is then put on a tiny boat and launched onto the river. It is a deep river with dangerous currents, and the tiny boat inevitably capsizes and the woman disappears. As a result, many families with daughters moved away from here."

"Well! Have you ever experienced flooding in this area?" the official asked.

"No, we have not. However, since the territory here is located in high land, we occasionally suffer drought."

"Hmm," the governor said. "Since the river deity is so powerful, I will make sure to attend this year's ceremony myself."

On the day of the marriage, the senior officials came to escort the governor to the ceremony. He was seated in a position of honor set up near the river and there they waited for the sorceress to arrive. Finally with great pomp and ceremony, the sorceress made her appearance. The governor assessed her as she approached. He saw an ugly, arrogant old woman. The monies she had collected over the years afforded her many luxuries, fine clothes, jewels, and an entourage of twenty female disciples

Before the ceremony could begin, the governor stood up. "As your new governor, allow me to say a few words, Your Grace," he said. "It is a great honor to be here, and on behalf of the county I would like to thank you for looking out for the best interests of the people. Clearly you have a powerful influence over the river deity. But, if I may say, I don't think this sacrificial lady is beautiful enough for the river deity. Perhaps we had better ask him if he likes this choice. Since you are the one to whom he speaks, it must of course be you who goes to ask."

Before the sorceress could argue, the governor motioned for his official to pick up the sorceress and throw her into the river. Everyone was shocked into silence. After a while, the governor said, "Why does it take her so long to take care of such a simple task? I think it's better for the three acolytes to check on her to see what is going on." Without hesitation, the three acolytes were thrown into the river.

"Three such awkward, clumsy representatives. There is no message from them either. We better send one of the sorceress's disciples to urge their return." His escorts immediately threw one disciple into the river. Again, no answer was received. The governor ordered that another two disciples be thrown into the river. The remaining disciples, realizing their fate, knelt down and begged for forgiveness.

After this event, the mysterious custom was stopped. News quickly traveled and the people returned.

Seven People Share Rice Soup
(七人分粥)

There were seven people living together. However, they had only one big bucket of rice soup each day to share among them, and there was never enough of the rice soup to fill up everyone's stomach.

In the beginning, they drew lots to choose who divided the soup. However, whoever was chosen always had a full stomach while the others were still hungry. Later, they chose the most respected among them to divide the soup. However, in order to receive more soup, each one of the others tried to please the chosen one. Soon, the group was full of politics, and they were all unhappy.

Next, they divided the seven people into two groups. One group of three would divide the soup, and the other four would judge how fairly the first group divided the soup. They argued and argued and took a long time to come to a conclusion. By the time they got to eat it, the rice soup was cold.

Finally, they came up with a method that worked. Each of the seven would take a turn dividing the soup. The one who divided the soup would get the last bowl.

Shu Zhan Saves the Country
(叔詹救國)

During the time of China's Spring and Autumn period (770–476 BCE) (春秋時代), there were many feudal lords who each controlled a part of the land and who frequently attacked one another.

In one such battle an army from the nation of Jin (晉) attacked the nation of Zheng (鄭), and the Zheng ruler sent a delegation to the Jin army to discuss conditions for their withdrawal. Duke Wen of Jin (636–627 BCE) (晉文公) made two demands: first, that the young Duke Lan (蘭) be set up as heir; second, that the minister Shu Zhan (叔詹), who opposed Duke Lan being made heir, be handed over to the Jin.

The Zheng ruler wanted to refuse the second condition. "If you go," the Zheng ruler said to his minister, "you will certainly die. I cannot bear to let you go."

"Jin has specified that it wants me. If I do not go, the Jin armies that now surround us certainly will not withdraw," Shu Zhan replied. "Isn't it my duty as minister to protect the people, and wouldn't I be showing myself to be afraid of death and insufficiently loyal if I remained in safety? What is so bad about letting a minister go to save the people and secure the nation?"

The ruler of Zheng, with tears in his eyes, called for some men to escort Shu Zhan to the Jin encampment.

When Duke Wen of Jin saw Shu Zhan, he immediately ordered that a large tripod be prepared to cook the minister to death. Shu Zhan, however, showed no fear.

"May I speak before you kill me?" he asked.

Duke Wen told him to speak quickly.

"Even as you attacked Zheng, I often praised your virtue and wisdom before others and thought that after you returned to Jin you would become the most powerful among the feudal lords. After the alliance negotiations at Wen (溫), I advised my lord to follow Jin. Unfortunately, he did not accept my suggestion. When you asked for me as a sacrifice for my kingdom, my lord refused to deliver me to you. I was the one who asked to come and save Zheng from danger. I am this kind of person. Accurately forecasting events is called wisdom, loving one's country with all one's heart is called loyalty, not fleeing in the face of danger is called courage, and being willing to die to save one's country is called benevolence. I find it hard to believe that a man of such qualities can be killed in Jin!"

Then, leaning against the tripod, he cried, "From this moment on, those who would serve this ruler should remember what happened to me!"

Duke Wen's expression changed after hearing this speech. He ordered that Shu Zhan be spared and had him escorted back to Zheng.

Snake Shadow on the Cup
(杯弓蛇影)

Sometimes we see something that bothers us and affects us deeply. Later, we may realize it was only our imagination.

When Dong Guang (東廣) was an officer in Henan Province (河南省), he invited a very close friend to his home for drinks. However, afterward, his friend didn't contact him for a long time. He wondered what could have happened to make his old friend stay away. One day he decided to go and see his friend.

When he arrived, he saw that his friend was seriously ill. He asked, "How did you get so sick? You were so healthy when you were in my home drinking."

"I did not want to tell you. You showed me such generous hospitality when you invited me to your home for drinks last time. But when I picked up my glass of wine to drink, I saw a little snake in the glass. I felt it was impolite to point it out and drank it. Since then, I became very sick."

Gong Guang remembered he had a sword hanging in the dining hall where they drank. On the scabbard, there was a painting of a snake. He believed that was the snake his friend saw. "I think I know the way to cure your sickness," Gong Guang said. "But you have to come to my home and drink with me again."

When they reached his home, Dong Guang positioned his friend in the same place he was the last time they were together and poured a glass of wine for him.

"Please pick up your glass. Can you see the snake again?" he asked.

"Yes, I see it," his friend answered.

Dong Guang then went to the sword and took it down. He asked again, "Still see the snake?"

"No, no. It is gone." When his friend realized that the snake he had seen was only an image of the painting on the sword hanging on the wall, his illness disappeared completely.

Spears and Shields against Each Other
(自相矛盾)

There was a merchant who sold shields and spears. In the market-place, he boasted, "My shields are so strong that nothing can pierce them. My spears are so sharp that there is nothing that cannot be pierced by them."

Someone in the crowd asked, "What will happen if you use one of your spears against one of your shields?"

The man could not offer any good answer.

Strange Human Thinking
(人間奇事)

A wise man once said, "Humans have strange behaviors. When they are young, they can't wait to grow up, and when they get old, they sigh that they have lost their childhood. When they are young, they use their health to earn money, and when they get old, they wish to use money to earn their health. They worry about the future but ignore the present happiness. Thus, they are not living in the present, nor living in the future. When they are alive, it seems they will never die, and when they are near death, it seems they have never had a life."

Swearing In a Corrupt Official
(貪官誓言)

There was a corrupt official who, in order to feign honesty and righteousness, took an oath in public, saying, "If my left hand accepts bribes, my left hand will fester, and if I accept bribes with my right hand, my right hand will fester."

One day, a businessman offered him one hundred pieces of gold as a bribe. He wanted to accept it but was afraid his oath would take effect.

His follower said, "Your Honor, why don't you ask the businessman to put the money in your sleeve? That way, if it will rot, it will be only your sleeve."

The official accepted the bribe.

The Borderline of Life and Death
(生死之界)

An old monk told a young monk, "When you were born to this world, you were crying, but all others were happy. However, when you are leaving this world, all others are crying, but you are happy. Therefore, death is not a cause for sorrow, and neither is birth a cause for happiness."

The Broken Wall
(破牆風波)

A prejudiced mind can fool you if you are not careful.

Once upon a time there was a rich man who owned a big house. One day there was a big hurricane. The winds knocked down a tree, which fell on the rich man's house and broke in a wall.

One of his neighbors came to comfort him and warned him to look out for thieves who might try to enter his house through the broken wall.

Later, his son also came to tell him to beware of thieves coming in through the broken wall.

Next morning, the rich man found that some money had been stolen out of his house. He suspected that his neighbor had taken it, and praised his son's wisdom.

The Carp in the Dry Track
(乾溝鯽魚)

Zhuang Zi (莊子) was poor and went to the Lord River Keeper to borrow some grain to avoid starvation.

"There is no problem. I shall soon receive taxes collected from my fief. After I receive the taxes, I will lend you three hundred gold nuggets. How about that?" said the River Keeper.

When Zhuang Zi heard this, he was very indignant but did not want to offend the River Keeper so he told him this story: "When I was coming here yesterday, I heard a voice calling me. I looked around and saw a carp in a dry track on the road.

"'How did you get here, carp?' I asked.

"'I am from the Eastern Ocean,' he said. 'I fell out of a fisherman's basket. He did not notice, and I was left here on this dry road. Do you have a bucket of water to save my life?'

"'No problem,' I said. 'I am on my way to visit the lord of Wu (吳) and Yue (越) in the south. I shall bring some water for you from the West River. How about that?'

"The carp said, 'I am out of my habitat and don't know what to do. One bucket of water now would save me. But you offer me nothing but an empty promise. When you return you will find me in the fish market.'"

The Cat and the Tiger
(貓與老虎)

Once upon a time a tiger met a cat. The tiger was amazed by the similarities between the cat and himself.

"Who are you?" the tiger asked.

The cat replied, "I am a cat like you, but I am the more evolved species of our kind."

"Liar!" the tiger shouted in anger.

"Ah-ha, tiger, my son, don't get angry. But it is no wonder that you are, for you are just too young, immature, and not yet evolved," the cat replied.

The tiger was insulted. "Cat," he said, "what are you talking about? I am too young and immature? Not evolved? Do you know that I can swallow you in one bite?"

The cat mewed, "Tiger, ah, don't get mad. It's not good for your health to get mad, but I guess you wouldn't understand because you are still too far down the ladder of evolution."

Growing impatient with the cat's words, the tiger began to scratch the ground with his paw and, snarling, showed his fearsome teeth. As he pounced, the tiger roared, "I am going to smash you in to pieces!"

The tiger struck at the cat with a swift and powerful movement. His paw landed with a loud sound.

The tiger laughed and said, "Ignorant cat, you dare to say that I am less evolved. What do you say now?"

The tiger was feeling quite happy with his abilities when he heard a mewing sound from behind. He looked back and was shocked to see the cat. The tiger lifted his paw. There was nothing but the deep imprint of his paw in the soil. The tiger tried not to show it, but he was clearly intimidated.

Perceiving the tiger's fear, the cat said, "Tiger, ah, you only have a slow and heavy body without any real martial techniques. Look at you. With all that power, all you could do was put a hole in the ground. You couldn't even touch me."

"What are martial techniques?" the tiger asked.

"Let me show you," the cat said. He then demonstrated his evasive jumping, rolling, spinning gongfu. Seeing this amazing display of ability, the tiger was humbled.

"What do you think, my less-evolved relative?" the cat asked.

The tiger, convinced by the cat's ability, knelt down before the cat and begged the cat to teach him. Seeing that the tiger was sincere, he agreed.

The tiger quickly learned the techniques the cat taught him. One day he said to the cat, "Hey, cat! I have learned all your techniques, I am not afraid of you anymore. If you should call me less evolved again, I will eat you for lunch."

The cat was outraged by what he heard, and said, "You unrighteous, immoral—"

Not waiting for the cat to finish, the tiger, using what he learned from the cat, began to attack. After they exchanged a few techniques, the cat felt that it was not worth the trouble to carry on the fight with the immoral tiger. The cat swiftly reached out and scratched the tiger on the nose and then used his technique called the spiritual cat climbs tree. He was up the tree in a flash.

The tiger had not learned this technique. He realized the cat had held back some of his teachings. Sitting on the branch, the cat said to the tiger with disgust, "Tiger, you will always be the less evolved cat of our species."

The Conceited Carriage Coachman
(自負馬夫)

One day the prime minister of Qi (齊), Yan Zi (晏子), went out with his carriage driven by his coachman. From her door, the coachman's wife saw her husband, looking conceited and sitting smugly under the carriage awning, driving the four horses.

When the coachman returned home, his wife asked for a divorce. Her husband asked her why.

"Yan Zi is the prime administer of Qi and well known throughout the country. But I saw him earlier riding in the carriage in deep thought and without airs. You are only his coachman, yet you looked so conceited and smug. This the reason I want to leave you," his wife answered.

After this exchange with his wife, her husband changed and became modest. Yan Zi noticed his coachman's new attitude and he asked the reason for the change. The coachman told him the truth. Later, Yan Zi promoted him and he became an officer.

The Chinese have a saying: "Satisfaction causes damage while humility receives benefit." (滿招損，謙受益。)

The Cunning of a Student
(學生之狡)

Once there was a proctor who was known to be very strict with students. One day, there was a student who committed a transgression and needed to be disciplined. The proctor sent for the student. He waited for a long time, and finally the student arrived. The student knelt down before him and said, "I am sorry I am late. I meant to come earlier. But I was distracted by the thousand pieces of gold I found, and I have had a hard time deciding how to dispose of them."

When the proctor heard about the gold, his temper decreased a little.

"Where did you find it?" he asked.

"It was buried under the ground, Sir," the student replied.

"And what are you going to do with it?" the proctor asked.

"Sir! I have discussed this with my wife and we agreed to spend four hundred hundreds pieces to buy land, two hundred for a house, one hundred for furniture, and one hundred to buy a servant. Then, I will use half of the remaining two hundred to buy books, and the remaining one hundred to offer you to remedy the trouble and headache I have caused in the past."

"Is it true? I don't think I deserve to share part of your fortune," the proctor said. Nevertheless, he ordered his cook to prepare a nice dinner for his student. They talked and toasted to each other's health.

When they were getting drunk, a concern for the gold occurred to the proctor.

"You came in such a hurry. Did you put the gold in a safe place?"

"Sir! I was busy planning how to use the money when my wife turned toward me and woke me up. I opened my eyes and all the gold was gone. Thus, I did not hide any of it," the student replied.

"So, all of what you are talking about was only a dream."

"Indeed, Sir!"

The proctor was angry at first, but since he had already shown his student hospitality, it would have been churlish to lose his temper with him. Besides, he had to admit to himself the student had a creative mind and might someday be an important politician.

He said, "I can see that, even in your dream, you kept me in mind. Remember, once you really acquire the gold, surely you will not forget me."

He urged the student to drink more wine with him.

A Broken Porcelain Bowl

An old man carried a basket of porcelain bowls on the street. Suddenly, one of the bowls fell to the ground and broke. He continued walking without stopping or even looking back.

"Why didn't you even take a look when your nice porcelain bowl fell on the ground and broke?" someone asked.

"Well, it would not matter how many times I looked back; the bowl would still be broken."

The Wisdom of a Child

There was a boy who went to a grocery store with his mother. When the owner saw this cute and polite boy, he said, "You may grab some candy from that jar."

The boy replied with a smile but did not move. After a few minutes, the owner offered again, but the boy just smiled at him without saying a word. Finally, the owner thought he was shy and used his hand to grab a big bunch of candy and gave it to the boy. The boy bowed and thanked the owner.

Later, after they left the store, his mom asked, "Why did you not take some candy when the owner asked you to?"

The boy replied, "His hand is bigger, so the candy he offered would be more." The mother praised his wisdom.

The Wisdom of Another Child

When a father was at work in his office, he received a phone call from his son.

"What's the problem?" he asked.

"Dad! I was playing baseball in the yard. Remember the big window near the living room?"

Before he continued, his father shouted in the phone, "Did you break that expensive window?"

"No, dad. I broke the small window next to it."

The Donkey Lover
(愛驢之人)

A rich, old miser made money by giving high-interest loans. When he got older and it was harder for him to walk, he bought a donkey to help him travel. But he became so fond of the donkey that he would not ride it unless he was extremely tired.

On a hot and sultry day, the old man needed to make a long journey, so he took the donkey with him. After walking for some distance, he was tired and short of breath. So, he mounted the donkey. After nearly three miles, the donkey was also short of breath because he was not used to being ridden. When the old man saw this, he dismounted and unsaddled the animal. However, the donkey thought he was being turned loose by his master. He took off and ran home.

Fearing the donkey might get lost and not willing to lose the saddle, he carried the saddle on his shoulders and hurried home. When he arrived home, he immediately asked his son if the donkey had returned. When the son told him the donkey had returned home safely, the old man was happy again. However, he was sick for nearly one month because of the exertion and heat stroke.

The End of the Guizhou Donkey
(黔驢技窮)

There were no donkeys in Guizhou (貴州) until someone brought one in by boat. But, later that person found there was no use for it and tied it up to a tree near the village.

A tiger was walking through the jungle. He hadn't caught anything to eat in days and was very hungry. Finally, he could stand it no longer. He was so hungry that he decided to leave the woods and go near the place where the humans lived to see if he could find something for his stomach.

When he came close to the village, he saw an animal he had never seen before. The animal must belong to the humans, he thought, since he was tied to a small tree by a leash attached to his nose.

The tiger thought that, because this strange animal belonged to the humans, he was probably very strong. He, therefore, approached the animal slowly and carefully.

When the donkey saw the tiger, he became afraid and started moving around violently. The tiger saw the power in the donkey's movements and felt this animal would not be easy for him to eat.

Since the animal was tied to a tree, the tiger decided that it was safe for him to get closer. As he did, the donkey became even more afraid and started kicking backward with his rear legs. The tiger concluded that the animal could only fight by kicking with his rear legs, just like many other animals. He began to feel braver and decided to play with the animal to see what other tricks and fighting abilities he might have.

He moved around the animal and waved his claws in front of the donkey's face. The donkey was so scared that he started to roar, "Neh! Neh!" The tiger now knew that the animal's second fighting trick was to make noise.

The tiger kept testing the animal and soon realized that he could only defend himself by kicking with his rear legs and making noise. He then jumped on the donkey's back and killed him. He had finally gotten a good meal.

What do you think about this story? Do you think that if the donkey had not shown his lousy fighting techniques, the tiger would have left him alone? Often it is better not to show what you know.

The Feeling of a General
(將軍錯覺)

A general was in his military tent on a cold winter night, drinking. Candles were lit and charcoal was burning in the stove for heat. After a few glasses of wine, he felt flush on his face and ears. He said, "What extraordinary weather we have this year. When it should be cold, it is warm."

The guard standing outside of the tent heard what the general had said. He entered the tent, knelt down respectfully in front of the general, and said, "Sir! The weather seems very normal where I was standing."

When we have plenty of food, we don't think there are many others who are starving. We should always put ourselves in others' position. This is at the heart of compassion.

The Fight of the Snipe
and the Mussel
(鷸蚌相爭)

When Zhao (趙) was about to attack Yan (燕), Su Dai (蘇代) spoke to King Hui of Zhao (趙惠王) on behalf of the Yan's king. He said, "On my way here today, as I crossed the Yi River (易水), I saw a mussel that opened his shell to sun itself. Suddenly, a snipe appeared and pecked at the flesh inside the mussel's shell. The mussel immediately closed his shell and seized the beak of the snipe so he could not get away.

"The snipe said, 'If there is no rain today or tomorrow, I will have a dead mussel.'

"But the mussel said, 'If you cannot escape from my grip today or tomorrow, it is you who will die from hunger.'

"Neither of them would give in to the other, and a fisherman came and snatched them both.

"If Zhao attacks Yan today, Yan and Zhao will resist each other for a long time and cause great suffering for their people. I am afraid that the fisherman will be mighty Qin (秦). For this reason, I hope your highness will take this matter in to consideration."

King Hui called off the attack.

The Fox Borrows the Tiger's Awe
(狐假虎威)

Very often, wisdom is more powerful than strength. Only if you study hard and keep learning will you become wise and successful.

One bright summer day, a certain fox was very hungry. He had spent the entire morning in his cave and decided to go out to catch some small animals to eat. A short time later, as he was walking down a path, a tiger crept up on him and caught him.

Before the tiger could eat him, the fox quickly calmed himself and hid his fear. He said loudly, "Wait, tiger! Don't you know you cannot eat me? I was sent to the earth by heaven to rule the animal world. If you eat me, you will be punished by heaven!"

When the tiger heard this, he began to laugh very loudly. He said, "I don't believe you, fox. You should be brave and accept your death." However, when he saw that the fox did not look terrified like all the other animals he caught, he was curious.

"You say you were sent by heaven to rule the animal world. Can you prove it?" the tiger asked.

The fox began to think that he might escape from the jaws of the tiger. He thrust out his chest, lifted his head, and said, "If you don't believe me, why don't we take a walk in the woods? You walk behind me to see how the other animals react when they see me."

The tiger was a little bit worried that perhaps the fox was telling the truth, so he decided to do what the fox said. After all, with him walking right behind, the fox wouldn't have a chance if he tried to escape. So, the two of them went for a walk in the woods.

When other animals saw the tiger as he walked behind the fox, they ran for their lives. However, to the tiger's eyes, it looked like all the animals were running away from the fox. He began to think the fox was telling the truth, and he became very afraid.

Without saying a word, the tiger turned and ran away. The clever fox had saved himself from the teeth of the tiger.

The Hunter's Fate
(獵人命運)

It is known that the deer is afraid of the wolf, the wolf is afraid of the tiger, and the tiger is afraid of the wild bear. The wild bear is the most ferocious and powerful of all animals, walking straight with long hair.

There was a hunter in Chu (楚) who knew how to blow a bamboo pipe to imitate the sounds of various animals. He often took his bow and arrows to the mountain to hunt deer. He used his bamboo pipe to lure the deer from their hiding place by mimicking their noise and then he would shoot them.

One day, he was hunting deer with his bamboo pipe. A wolf heard the pipe, thought it was a deer, and came to investigate. The hunter saw the wolf and, frightened, he imitated the roar of a tiger. The wolf ran away, but a tiger appeared. Terrified, he immediately blew the bamboo pipe imitating the bear. The tiger ran away, but suddenly a bear appeared. The bear found it was a man, not a tiger, so it tore him apart and ate him.

The Innocent Fawn
(愚蠢小鹿)

A man in Linjiang (臨江) captured a fawn and brought it home. When his dogs saw it, they came licking their chops and wagging their tails. The man got angry and drove them away. Later, he took the fawn and let it stay with the dogs while warning them to keep peace with one another. Not too long afterward, the dogs learned their lesson. As the fawn grew, it gradually forgot that it was a deer and considered all dogs to be friends with whom it could play. The dogs, fearful of their master, suppressed their natural instinct and fraternized with the deer.

Three years later, the deer went outside the gate. It found there were some strange dogs outside and tried to play with them. The dogs were surprised but delighted that a nice meal was coming to them. They fell upon it and killed it.

The Lamb in Tiger Skin
(羊蒙虎皮)

Once there was a lamb that put on a tiger skin. As it was roaming around in a nice meadow and enjoying the green grass, it saw a wolf in the distance. It was so frightened and trembled all over. It forgot that it had the tiger skin on its body.

Using tiger skin to hide your identity is temporary. The truth is that you cannot hide yourself under cover forever.

The Lord of Yan Looking for Longevity
(燕王求壽)

There was a stranger who came to see the Lord of Yan (燕王) and told him he knew the way to immortality. The lord was very happy and asked one of his close and trusted officers to learn from this stranger. Unfortunately, before this officer could learn from him, the stranger died. The lord was so angry that he executed the officer.

How stupid of the lord! He could not see the truth that the stranger was cheating him, and blamed his officer instead. This stranger could not even keep himself alive. How could he teach the lord the method of immortality?

The Lord Who Loved Dragons
(葉公好龍)

Lord Ye was very fond of dragons. He had them painted on the walls and carved all over the house. A real dragon heard about this. It flew down and placed its head through Lord Ye's door and its tail through his window. When Lord Ye saw this, he was so frightened he fled from the house.

The Lost Ax
(農夫失釜)

Once there was a farmer who one day lost his ax. He suspected that a neighbor's boy had stolen it, but he couldn't prove it.

From that day on, whenever he saw the boy, he thought that the boy looked like a thief, walked like a thief, and talked like a thief.

Two weeks later, the farmer found the ax in his barn, right where he had left it. From that time on, whenever he saw the boy, the farmer thought he looked, talked, and walked just like any other boy.

The Love of the Kingfisher
(翠鳥之愛)

The kingfisher is a timid bird. It always builds its nest on the top of a tall tree for protection against danger. Later, when fledglings hatch, it is afraid that the newborn will fall from the tree. Thus, it moves the nest lower down. When their feathers begin to appear, it becomes even more concerned and scared so it moves the nest even lower. The kingfisher moves its nest so low that anything is now able to catch them.

The Owl Moves His Home
(鴞鳥搬家)

One day, an owl told a dove that he would move away from where he lived. The dove asked, "Why are you going to move?"

"All the people around here do not like my hoot," the owl replied.

"Then where will you move?" the dove asked.

"I will move to the east," the owl replied.

"I believe it is best if you can change your voice instead of moving," said the dove. "If you don't change your voice, then it does not matter if you move to the east. The people there will be just the same as the people here."

The Poison of Love
(愛之毒藥)

A long time ago there was a girl named Li-Li (麗麗). Li-Li got married and went to live with her husband and mother-in-law. To her dismay, Li-Li found she couldn't get along with her mother-in-law at all. Their personalities were very different, and Li-Li was infuriated by many of her mother-in-law's habits, especially her habit of criticizing Li-Li constantly.

Days passed, then weeks passed, and Li-Li and her mother-in-law never stopped arguing and fighting. But what made the situation worse is that, according to ancient Chinese tradition, Li-Li had to bow to her mother-in-law and obey her every wish. All the anger and unhappiness in the house was causing the husband great distress.

Finally, Li-Li could not stand her mother-in-law's bad temper and dictatorship any longer and decided to do something about it. Li-Li went to see her father's good friend Mr. Huang (黃先生), who was an herbalist. She told him the problem and asked if he would give her some poison so that she could solve the problem once and for all.

Mr. Huang thought for a while and finally said, "Li-Li, I will help you."

Li-Li said, "Thank you, Mr. Huang, I will do whatever you tell me to do."

Mr. Huang went into the back room and returned in a few minutes with a package of herbs. He told Li-Li, "You can't use a quick-acting poison to get rid of your mother-in-law because that would cause people to become suspicious. Therefore, I have given you a number of herbs that will slowly build up poison in her body. Every other day prepare some pork or chicken and put a little of these herbs in her serving. Now, in order to make sure that nobody suspects you when she dies, you must be very careful to act very friendly toward her. Don't argue with her, obey her every wish, and treat her like a queen."

Li-Li was so happy. She thanked Mr. Huang and hurried home to start the process of murdering her mother-in-law.

Weeks passed, then months passed, and every other day Li-Li served the specially treated food to her mother-in-law. She remembered what Mr. Huang had said about avoiding suspicion, so she controlled her temper, obeyed her mother-in-law, and treated her like her own mother.

After six months, the harmony of the household changed. Li-Li had practiced controlling her temper so much that she found that she almost never got mad or upset. She hadn't had an argument with her mother-in-law in six months. In fact her mother-in-law seemed much kinder and easier to get along with. Her attitude toward Li-Li had changed, and she began to love Li-Li like her own daughter. She kept telling friends and relatives that Li-Li was the best daughter-in-law one could ever find. Li-Li and her mother-in-law were now treating each other just like a real mother and daughter. Li-Li's husband was very happy to see what was happening.

One day Li-Li rushed over to see Mr. Huang and again asked for his help. She said, "Dear Mr. Huang, please help me to keep the poison from killing my mother-in-law! She's changed into such a nice woman, and I love her like my own mother. I do not want her to die because of the poison I gave to her."

Mr. Huang smiled and nodded his head.

"Li-Li," he said, "there's nothing to worry about. I never gave you any poison. All of the herbs I gave you were simply to improve her health. The only poison was in your mind, but that has been all washed away by the love you gave to her."

The Repentance of an Old Man
(老人懺悔)

An old man sat next to his wife in the hospital. His wife had just had a stroke and was in a coma. He did not know what to do.

"My dear love! Please wake up." He was filled with grief and tears welled in his eyes. He kept calling his wife.

He remembered that they had a dream to travel to Europe ever since they knew each other. However, when they had first met, they were just college students and did not have money to travel.

After they got married, they had three children. They spent all their time earning money so the children had what they needed. When the children entered college, they thought of traveling to Europe. However, his business was on the rise, and he could not find any spare time for the trip, not to mention having time to take a walk to the park. He remembered he told her, "Wait till I am retired. We will have all the time in the world to travel."

He had just retired, but his wife couldn't wait.

"My dear, please wake up. I want to take you to Paris, Rome, London . . ."

The Retribution of the Merchant
(賈人報應)

Once upon a time, there was a woman who lived with her son. They were very poor. To support the family, the son grew vegetables and carried them to the market for sale. It was hard work and he made very little money.

One day, as this young man was returning from the market-place, he urgently had to relieve himself. He quickly found a public lavatory. After he finished, he discovered an unattended bag on the corner. Curious, he opened it. To his surprise, he found fifty gold nuggets in the bag. He thought about the person who lost the gold and how very worried that person would be. Maybe this person was intending to use this money to pay for some urgent necessities. So, he waited there with the bag. He waited for a few hours until almost sunset.

At last he saw a man hurrying to the lavatory. The man was obviously looking for something. The young man walked forward and asked, "Mister, did you lose something?"

"Yes, young man, I lost an important bag somewhere and I can't find it." The merchant replied. The young man then took out the bag from his vegetable basket and asked, "Is this the one you lost?"

When the merchant saw the bag, he was relieved and appreciative for its return. He happily took the bag. However, his appreciation lasted only for a short time. He realized that if he admitted this bag was his, he would have to reward this young man for his honesty. However, if he did not admit it, this bag would belong to the young man. He opened the bag and counted the gold nuggets. "Wait a minute," he said, "I had one hundred gold nuggets in this bag. Why is it now only fifty?"

He demanded the young man return the other fifty gold nuggets. Naturally, the young man was not able to do that. Finally, they went to the courthouse.

After listening to both sides, the judge concluded that the merchant had intended to take advantage of the honest young man. He realized that if the young man had intended to keep the money, he would not have stayed at the lavatory waiting for the bag's owner.

The judge decided to teach the merchant a lesson. He asked, "Sir, did you say you had one hundred gold nuggets in the bag?"

"Yes, Your Honor," the merchant replied.

The judge then asked the young man, "Did you say, when you found this bag, there were only fifty gold nuggets in the bag?"

"It is true, Your Honor," the young man answered.

The judge then told the merchant, "Since the bag you lost had one hundred gold nuggets inside, and the bag this young man found had only fifty gold nuggets, I believe that this bag does not belong to you, but to someone else. I will keep this bag for two days, and if no one comes to claim his loss, this bag and the fifty gold nuggets should belong to this young man."

The merchant was shocked. However, he could not offer any argument. Of course, no one came to claim the bag. The bag and its fifty gold nuggets were given to the young man.

The Thief and the Bell
(小偷與鐘)

Many years ago in a village in China, many merchants got together for a big business meeting. After the meeting, they had a great feast. One of the merchants was about to depart on a trip to buy new merchandise and had all the money he owned in his coat pocket. Since he was with his fellow businessmen, he thought it would be safe if he left it in his coat with all the others in a room next to the dining room.

When the meeting ended and it was time to go home, he discovered that someone had stolen all of his money. This was a disaster. He needed the money to buy new merchandise. If he couldn't do this, he would go out of business. He would even have trouble surviving! There was nothing else he could do, so he went to the local judge for help.

In ancient China, the local judge was the highest official in the area, and he was also the chief of police. The judge called together all of the merchants who had been at the meeting. He told them what had happened and said, "This is a very unfortunate matter, but I'm confident that I will be able to quickly bring the thief to justice."

He sipped a mouthful of tea and continued. "Several years ago I obtained a mysterious bell from a Daoist priest. This bell will recognize the thief and point him out to me."

He led the merchants to a curtain with a slit in it.

"Behind this curtain," he said, "is the bell I told you about. It contains very powerful magic, and I have to keep it covered for your protection. I order you now to go to the curtain one at a time, put your hand through the slit in the curtain, and push the bell. When people who are innocent of this theft push the bell, it will not make any sound, but if the guilty man touches it, even lightly, it will ring loudly and we will all know that he is the thief."

One by one, the merchants went up to the curtain and put a hand through the slit. However, when all of them had taken their turns, the bell still had not rung.

The judge then ordered all of the merchants to line up in front of him and hold out their hands. After he had inspected all of them, he pointed to one of them and said, "You are the thief!" and ordered the guard to arrest him.

Everyone in the court was shocked and wondered how the judge could know this merchant was the thief. The judge stood up and explained, "Actually, the bell wasn't magic at all. It's just a regular bell. I tied up the clapper so that it wouldn't ring no matter how hard it was pushed, and I covered the outside of the bell with ink. I know that everyone with a clear conscience would not hesitate to push the bell, but the thief wouldn't dare touch it even lightly. After everyone had gone to the curtain, I simply looked to see who didn't have any ink on his hands."

Everyone in the court applauded the wisdom of the judge.

The Mask of the King
(國王面具)

Do you have a mask on your face? Is what you show people on your face what you really think? Do we have to wear a mask in today's society? How heavy and how thick is your mask? Have you ever taken your mask off and taken a good look at the real you in the mirror? If you can do this, it will make you humble. Then, even if you have a mask on your face, your life will not be ruled by your mask.

Long, long ago there was a king who lived in Asia. Nobody had ever seen the king's real face. Whenever he met with his ministers and officials or appeared in public, he always wore a mask. The face on the mask had a very stern and solemn expression.

Because nobody could see the real expression on his face, all the officials and people respected him, obeyed him, and feared him. This made it possible for him to rule the country efficiently and well.

One day his wife said to him, "If you have to wear the mask in order to rule the country, then what the people respect and obey is the mask and not you."

The king wanted to prove to his wife that it was he who really ruled the country and not the mask. He decided to take the mask off and let the officials see his real face.

Without the mask, the officials were able to see the expression on his face and figure out what he was thinking. It wasn't long before the officials weren't afraid of him anymore.

A few months passed and the situation got steadily worse. He had lost the solemn dignity that made people fear him and, even worse, the officials had started to lose respect for him. Not only did they argue with one another in front of him, but they even began to argue with him about his decisions.

He soon realized that the unity and cooperation among his officials had disintegrated. His ability to lead the country had gradually disappeared and the country was falling to disorder. The king realized that in order to regain the respect of the people and his ability to rule the country, he had to do something. He gave the order to behead all of the officials who had seen his face, and he appointed new ones. He then put the mask back on his face. Soon afterward, the country was again united and under his control.

The Value of a Horse
(雇專相馬)

Only those who lack self-confidence trust other people's judgment more than their own. The best way to gain this confidence is to become knowledgeable through reading and learning.

A thousand years ago, there was a young man whose name was He Su (何溯). Although he was very poor, he owned a very nice horse that his father had given him before he died. He Su needed money to live on so he sold almost all of his belongings except for his horse.

Finally, in order to save himself from starvation, he decided to sell his horse. However, because he was so poor and hadn't been able to feed the animal properly, the horse was skinny and didn't look very good.

He took his horse to the horse market every day, but after two weeks nobody had even asked him the price. He became very worried. At last he thought of a way he might be able to sell the horse.

The next morning, he visited the best-known horseman of the time, a man named Ying Wei (嬰偉) and asked for his help in selling the horse. He requested that Ying Wei come to the horse market to see his horse. He did not have to buy the horse but just take a good look at the horse, walk around him a few times, and when he was leaving, look back at the horse a couple times. If Ying Wei could do this for him, he would give him one-third of what he got for the horse.

Ying Wei agreed, and the next morning he appeared at the horse market. He was well known, and so everybody noticed him. As requested, he looked around and finally came to He Su. He took a look at He Su's horse, circled the horse a few times, and as he was leaving, he looked back at the horse a couple of times. Then he went home.

That afternoon, He Su sold his horse for three times what he was worth.

The Warning of a Wild Goose Sentry
(雁奴報警)

When a flock of wild geese gathers together, the smallest and the most alert one is often chosen to keep vigil for the others at night. If there is the slightest abnormal sound, the goose raises the alarm, and the flock will wake up from its sleep and take off.

One group of wild-goose hunters devised a scheme to trick the sentry. First, they marked the haunt of the flock and spread a huge net around and hid themselves nearby. When night came, the flock descended and went to sleep. When it got dark, the hunters lit a torch. As soon as the sentry noticed it and gave warning, they immediately extinguished the torch. The flock was startled, but when they saw nothing was happening and that it was quiet, they went back to sleep.

The hunters performed the same trick three times. The third time, the flock thought the sentry was giving a false alert and pecked him for punishment. Again, they went back to sleep.

After a while, the hunters lit the torch again, but the sentry remained silent this time. While the flock continued sleeping, the hunters drew in the net and captured more than half the flock.

Three Metaphors on Study
(好學比喻)

One day, Duke Pin of Jin (晉文公) said to his blind musician Shi Kuang (師曠), "I am seventy already. Though I still want to study and read, I think it is too late."

"Then why don't you light a candle and use its light?" Shi Kuang suggested.

"How dare you joke with your master?" the duke asked in anger.

Shi Kuang replied, "As a blind musician and courtier, I dare not joke with you. However, I heard that when you are young and like to study, it is like the rising sun. When you are middle-aged and like to study, it is like the sun at noon. If you like to study when you are old, it is like a candle flame. Though the candle is not very bright, at least it is better than fumbling in the darkness."

Three Monks
(三個和尚)

Once upon a time, there was a small abandoned temple on a mountain. One day, a small monk who went to visit the temple decided to move in. When he saw there was no water in the water tank, he went to get water from a stream and filled up the tank. He also filled up the water in the jar next to Bodhisattva, Guanyin (觀音). The dried willow branches in the jar revived. Daily, he got water, chanted while knocking wood fish (for chanting), and kept mice from stealing his food. He lived there peacefully and happily.

Not too long thereafter, along came a tall monk. He was very thirsty and, once he arrived, he finished the remaining half tank of water. The small monk asked him to get more water from the stream, but the tall monk thought it was not fair for him to do this by himself, so he demanded that the small monk go get the water with him. Both of them went to pick up the water with a bucket and a pole. After they filled the bucket, they placed it at the middle of the pole to carry it back to the temple. However, due to their different heights, the bucket always slid to the end of the pole held by the small monk. Finally, they decided to take turns getting the water.

Later, a fat monk came to the temple. He was also thirsty and wanted to drink water. Unfortunately, there was no more water in the tank. The small monk and tall monk asked him to pick up the water. Once he brought the water back, he finished it completely, by himself.

After that, no one would go to pick up the water willingly. All three monks went thirsty.

Every day, the three chanted and knocked the wood fish individually. The jar next to Bodhisattva, Guanyin, remained empty and the

willow branch withered. When mice came out to steal food, no one cared. One night, one of the mice knocked down the candle and triggered a fire.

The three monks panicked and helped one another extinguish the fire. They all woke up and realized they must cooperate with one another. After that, the jars of drinking water were always full.

Two Children Discuss the Sun
(二童論日)

One day, Confucius was taking a walk when he saw two children arguing. He went to see if he could help settle their dispute.

"Why are you quarreling?" asked the great scholar.

One child said, "I think the sun is closer to us in the morning and farther away at midday. My friend thinks that the sun is closer at midday and farther away in the morning."

Confucius listened with great interest and asked, "What are your reasons for thinking these things?"

The first child said, "In the morning the sun is as big as the wheel of a cart. At noon, it's as small as a plate. It must be because it is closer in the morning and farther away later!"

"No!" the second child said. "The sun is hotter at noon than in the morning, and if it is hotter, then it must be closer!"

Confucius was very impressed with their reasoning, but didn't know how to decide who was right. When the children saw that Confucius couldn't give them an answer, they laughed loudly and said, "Who says you are a man of great learning?" Still laughing, they skipped away together.

Wipe Windows for Five Years
(五年擦窗)

Success does not depend on how smart you are but on your level of discipline. Doing good work always earns trust. Trust is the key to successful relationships.

Due to his poor family background, Xiaohua (小華) only finished his junior-high education because he needed to work to help his family. One day he decided to go to the city to find a way to earn more income. He soon found a job in a window-cleaning company. All he earned was seventy dollars a month.

Some friends asked him, "Why don't you find a way to complete your higher education? If you do, you could find a better job with higher pay."

"My family is so poor, and they have already provided me with an education through junior high school. Now, I need to earn some money to help them. Though the money I earn is not much, it provides me food and lodging in the city, and I have some extra to send home to help my family. My life is very good here."

Cleaning windows is not an easy job. It is physically demanding and often dangerous. It requires balancing on a scaffold high in the air, and sometimes the scaffolding is poorly made. Many people who worked in the same job did not last even six months. However, Xiaohua continued to find ways to do his job better and faster. He always made sure his scaffolding was in good order so there was never any delay on his jobs. He developed good techniques so his windows were always the cleanest and done in the fastest time. He worked hard and did the jobs without complaint. With his good attitude and personal happiness, all the customers liked and trusted him. Soon, he was known as the "Window Cleaning Boy." In a year, he was able to leave the company and start his own business. People knew if they hired Window Cleaning Boy they could trust him to get the job done. All the while he continued to save whatever money he could. He had a plan.

Five years later, he was ready. The money he saved he used to open a healthy fast-food restaurant on a corner of a busy street. Over the years he had learned from the people in the buildings he cleaned that a healthy fast-food restaurant was exactly what people wanted and needed in that busy business district. Due to the good relationships he had developed with all his previous window-cleaning customers, his business took off in just a few months. He became a successful businessman despite his impoverished background. A few years later, he owned ten healthy fast-food restaurants.

When journalists of daily newspapers interviewed him to learn the reason for his success, he said, "It was because I worked as a window cleaner for five years and I did a good job."

Zeng Shen Kills Someone
(曾參殺人)

Other people can often influence our thinking. Even when we have a firm mind, we can still be influenced, especially if there are several people who are saying the same thing. This may also happen when we have lost self-trust. We ask others' opinions and then follow their advice. However, we always forget the fact that is no one knows you better than yourself. Why do we trust someone else instead of ourselves?

Once there was a man named Zeng Shen (曾參) who lived with his mother in the county of Fei (費). There was a man who had the same name as Zeng Shen, and he committed a murder. Someone rushed to the first Zeng Shen's mother, who was weaving cloth, and said, "Zeng Shen just killed a man!"

"I don't believe my son would do that," she said and continued her weaving.

After a while, another person came and told her, "Zeng Shen has just killed a man!"

Still, she went on her weaving without saying a word.

Then a third person came and shouted to her, "Zeng Shen has killed a man!" This time his mother was frightened and she threw down her shuttle and rushed to find the truth.

Zeng Shen Kills the Pig
(曾參殺豬)

When Zeng Shen's wife was going to the market, their son was crying and following her.

"Go back," she told him. "When I return, I will kill a pig for your supper."

Later, when she returned, she found Zeng Shen about to kill a pig. She quickly stopped him.

"I didn't mean it when I said I was going to kill a pig. I just said it to keep the boy quiet and so he would return home," she explained.

"How can you deceive a child like that?" Zeng Shen asked. "Children know nothing at the beginning. They just copy their parents and learn from them. When you lie to the boy, you are teaching him to lie. If a mother deceives her child, he will not trust her anymore. This is not the way to teach a child."

His wife, humbled, helped Zeng Shen kill the pig for the child.

Zhang, San-Feng Teaches Taiji Sword (三豐教劍)

When you learn any skill from a master, you are learning both the basic concept and the master's experience and feeling. After you have mastered the skills with your own feeling, you will be able to create new art. Then you will be a real artist.

The famous taijiquan master, Zhang, San-Feng (張三豐), had a talented and dedicated student. The student studied the art of the taijiquan sword with Master Zhang for three years. At the end of the three years Master Zhang was very happy and said, "Now that you have learned the feeling of this sword art from me, it is time for you to go home to practice by yourself. After you practice three years, come back to see me."

The student went home and practiced day and night. After three years, as promised, the student went to see Master Zhang. When he arrived, Master Zhang could see he was uneasy and embarrassed. "What has happened? Did you not practice hard what you have learned from me?" Master Zhang asked.

"Yes, master! I practiced very hard, every day. However, after three years of practice, I have found that I have lost 30 percent of the feeling I learned from you. I am sorry, master." The student bowed.

Master Zhang looked at him with sincere eyes, "No good! No good! Go home and practice another three years, and then come to see me."

The student left feeling more pressure this time. He practiced even harder than ever. However, after three years, when he went to see Master Zhang, his head bowed even lower than before. He said, "Master Zhang! I am very sorry. I have practiced every day and every night for three more years, but now I feel that nearly

70 percent of the movements are not the same as I learned from you."

Master Zhang looked at him and said, "No good! No good! Go home and practice another three years, and then come to see me."

The student left with a deeply humbled mind. He practiced and practiced ceaselessly. However, after another three years, when he faced Master Zhang, he knelt down to the ground, "Master Zhang, I am really sorry. Now, I don't have the same feeling for any movement as I learned from you."

Master Zhang looked at him with his shining eyes and said, "Good! Good! Now, it is not mine anymore. It is yours."

Zou Ji Compares His Beauty
(鄒忌比美)

Lord Zou Ji (鄒忌), who lived in the state of Qi (齊), was six feet tall and very handsome. One morning as his wife helped him dress in beautiful clothes and a nice hat, he looked in the mirror and asked his wife, "Who is more handsome, Lord Xu (徐公) of the north city, or I?"

"You are very handsome. How can Lord Xu compare with you?" his wife replied.

Lord Zou did not believe it since Lord Xu was well known throughout the state for his handsome looks. He sought out his concubine and asked her the same question.

"How can Lord Xu compare with you?" his concubine answered.

The next day a guest came to visit him. He asked the guest the same question.

"Lord Xu is not as good looking as you," the guest said.

One day Lord Xu came to visit him personally. Lord Zou took a close look him. After Lord Xu left, he looked in the mirror and studied his own face. He felt he was not as handsome as Lord Xu. That night, in bed the truth came to him. He thought, "My wife said I am more handsome than Lord Xu because she is biased in favor of me. My concubine said it because she is afraid of me. My guest said so because he wants something from me."

Thirty Years of More Mistakes
(再錯三十)

An old master was terribly sad and was crying. His student came up to him to ask why he was so sad. He said, "After thirty years of cultivation and training, I've realized I have learned almost nothing."

The student said, "Master, is that not good? Since you realize you have learned almost nothing, now it is the time to learn something. Therefore, you should be happy."

However, the master continued to cry. The student again asked why. The master said, "I am afraid that after another thirty years I will still have learned nothing."

The Trick of Gold

This is another story from my White Crane master.

A long time ago, there was an old master who could change an ordinary rock into a piece of gold. Many poor people came to him and asked if he had any extra little pieces of gold lying around they might have. The kind old man never disappointed them, and he helped them all as much as he could.

One day, a twelve-year-old boy came to see him. The boy said, "Honorable master! I heard that you can change a rock into a piece of gold. Is this true?"

The old master replied, "Yes, it is. Do you want a piece of gold like the others? If you do, I will change a rock into gold for you."

"Oh no, Honorable master," said the boy, "I do not want the gold. What I would like from you, if you permit, is your trick for changing rocks into gold."

The master realized this boy was different from all others, and he smiled. The boy realized that if the old man gave him a piece of gold, it would soon be spent. However, if he knew how to make the gold himself, he would have enough gold for the rest of his life.

A Master's Answer

There was once a man of reputed wisdom. A younger man, seeking to get the better of the wise one, captured a bird and held it firmly in his hand to keep the bird still. Taking it to the elder, he asked this question, "Master, is this bird I hold alive or dead?"

The young man intended to set the bird free if the master answered that it was dead and to crush the bird in his hands if the master said it was alive. In this way the young man hoped to discredit the master while advancing his own reputation.

The master looked carefully into the young man's eyes and said, "The answer is in your hands."

Two Make One
(瞎子跛子)

When marauding bandits attacked a village, a lame man told a blind man they could help each other escape. The blind man carried the lame man on his back, and the lame man provided his eyesight to guide them both to safety. Together they evaded the bandits and lived.

Confucius said: "If there are three persons walking together, there will always be one among them who can be my teacher." (三人行必有我師。) Different individuals have different talents and expertise. If we could all share and coordinate our talents to help each other, the world would become a more harmonious and peaceful place.

A Swordsman's Revenge

Forgiveness is not easy. However, if you forgive, your life will be peaceful and harmonious. The Chinese have a saying: "One step backward, the ocean is big and the sky is wide" (退一步，海闊天空).

At dinner one evening long ago, a twelve-year-old boy was eating with his family. Suddenly, a samurai burst into the house and began killing everyone. During the chaos, the boy hid himself in a closet in an obscure corner of the room. The boy was very frightened and dared not make any noise. From a tiny hole in the closet door, he saw his grandma, father, mother, brothers, and sisters die one by one. He could see this murderer's face very clearly. When the swordsman killed everyone, he left.

The boy, orphaned and a beggar, traveled around the country and searched for the best samurai master in the country. He was accepted as a disciple of a master and practiced day and night. All that was in his mind was revenge for his family. This obsession empowered him, and in twelve years he became one of the best swordsmen in Japan.

After he completed his training, he traveled to every corner of Japan searching for the man who had killed his family. He searched and searched. Many years went by and still there was no sign of his enemy. He was discouraged and saddened. Twenty years passed and still he could not find his enemy. Yet his desire for revenge never decreased.

One day, he came upon a turbulent stream in a remote mountain area. There was no bridge connecting one side to the other. As he looked for a good place to cross, he saw an old man carrying a log. When he stepped forward to help him, he was jolted to a standstill. This old man was the enemy he had been looking for these past twenty years.

Without saying a word, he drew his sword. But before he executed the old man he wanted the old man to know why. He told the old man exactly which day and what time he had killed his entire family. When the old man heard the story, he immediately knelt down and admitted the crime. He looked into the young swordsman's eyes and said, "I am very sorry to have committed such a crime. You deserve to kill me in revenge. But before I die, may I make a request?"

"Say it," the young swordsman replied.

"The bridge here was washed away by the big flood last year. The people of the village cannot cross the river easily, and it is a hardship for many to walk miles downstream for a safe place to cross. As an act of atonement I would like to build this bridge. If you permit me, please allow me to finish the bridge before you take my life."

Since what the old man was doing was a good deed, the young swordsman agreed to wait.

The young swordsman built a tent next to the river so he could watch the old man day and night to prevent him from escaping. He waited patiently, but the old man's progress was very slow. After six months, he got up to help the old man carry logs. Soon, they were working together. In order to coordinate their efforts, they began to talk to each other and got to know each other better.

After three years, the bridge was completed. In the evening, the old man washed his body and came to the young swordsman's tent. He knelt down in front of the young man and said, "Now, the bridge is completed. Thank you for your help and allowing me to finish it. It is time to receive my retribution." The old man kept his head down and prepared to be beheaded.

The young swordsman kept quiet for a while and pondered. Finally, he knelt down in front of the old man.

"I cannot kill you," he said. "My life was miserable in the past. It was filled with hate and anger. The last three years building the bridge with you has brought me the first peace and calmness I have felt in too many years. I cannot kill you. If I do, I will kill my second life." The young man spoke with tears in his eyes.

Together the two men, now friends, traveled the country.

Bai-Yin the Monk

Monk Bai-Yin (白隱禪師) was reputed to be a very respectable monk. In the neighboring village, there was a young woman who lived with her parents. One day, the father discovered his daughter was pregnant. The father was angry and demanded his daughter tell him who was the father of the child. The girl was afraid that her father would kill the man she loved. She also knew her father respected monk Bai-Yin deeply. So she told her parents that the father of the child was Bai-Yin.

The father was shocked and couldn't believe that the respectable monk Bai-Yin was such a miserable person. He took a staff and went to see Bai-Yin.

"You are such an evil person," he said. "Why did you do it with my daughter?"

"What did I do with your daughter?" Bai-Yin asked.

"Don't you dare deny it. You bastard!"

Bai-Yin listened quietly. After a while, he understood the situation. He said, "Oh! Is it so?" He did not deny it or try to defend himself. He knew it was impossible to argue with an outraged father.

After the child was born, the father took the child to Bai-Yin. He believed it was his responsibility to look after the child. Everyone in the town knew what was happening. Bai-Yin had lost their respect and his reputation was tarnished. Nevertheless, Bai-Yin worked very hard to care for the child. He did not complain or explain to anyone. He took care of the child with his heart.

One year passed, and the daughter could not stand her guilt anymore; she revealed the truth to her parents. After her parents listened to the truth, they were ashamed and filled with regret. They went to the temple and begged Bai-Yin's forgiveness. After Bai-Yin listened to their apology without anger, he returned the child to his mother. He had come to love the child, but once again chose in the best interest of the child.

After this event, all the people respected Bai-Yin even more than ever.

Destiny of Coin Tossing

The great Japanese general Nobunaga, in spite of being outnumbered ten to one, decided to attack. He felt sure of victory, but his soldiers were very doubtful. As they prepared for battle, they stopped at a Buddhist temple. Nobunaga prayed, and as he was leaving the sanctuary said, "I am going to throw a coin up into the air. If it is heads, we will win; if it is tails, they will destroy us. Destiny will show us its faith, and we will know our destiny."

He tossed the coin up, and it came down heads. The soldiers, with a renewed confidence and high spirit, defeated their enemies in spite of being outnumbered.

The next day, the aide-de-camp said to Nobunaga, "Nothing can change our destiny."

"Yes," answered Nobunaga, showing him the fake coin with heads on both sides. Power of prayer? Power of destiny? Or the power of belief?

The Full Cup

Once upon a time a student came to see a Zen master. He said, "Honorable master, I have studied many years. I have learned the skills of the martial arts and understand Zen theory. I have reached a very high level. I heard you are a great master, and I have, therefore, come to see if you can teach me anything more."

The master didn't reply. Instead, he picked up a teacup and placed it in front of the student, then picked up the teapot and began to pour the tea. He poured until the tea reached the rim of the cup and kept

on pouring until the tea overflowed onto the table. The student stared at the master in total confusion and said, "No! No! Master, the tea is overflowing!"

The master stopped pouring, looked at him, and smiled. He said, "Young man, this is you. I am sorry that I cannot accept you as a student. Like this cup, your mind is filled up, and I cannot teach you any more. If you want to learn, you must first empty your cup."

The Chinese have a saying: "Satisfaction loses and humility gains." (滿招損，謙受益。)

Heaven and Hell

The bold and handsome young Samurai warrior stood respectfully before the aged Zen master and said, "Master, teach me about heaven and hell."

The master snapped his head up in disgust and said, "Teach you about heaven and hell? I doubt you could even learn to keep your own sword from rusting, you ignorant fool. How dare you suppose you could understand anything I might have to say?"

The old man went on and on, becoming even more insulting, while the young swordsman's surprise turned first to confusion, then to hot anger, rising by the minute. Master or not, who dares insult a Samurai and live?

At last, with teeth clenched and blood nearly boiling in fury, the warrior blindly drew his sword and prepared to end the old man's life and silence his sharp tongue all in one moment.

The master looked straight into his eyes and said gently, "That is hell."

At the peak of his rage, the Samurai realized the master had bound him into a living hell, driven by uncontrolled anger and ego. That was his teaching.

The young man, profoundly humbled, sheathed his sword and bowed to this great spiritual teacher. Looking up into the wise man's aged, beaming face, he felt more love and compassion than he had ever felt in his life. The master raised his index finger, and said, "And that is heaven."

A Lesson to the Prince

Once there was a wise king in Korea who had a fifteen-year-old son. This son had grown up in the luxury of the palace with all the attention of many servants. This worried the king. He believed his son was too pampered and would never be a good king whose concern was for his people. He decided to summon a well-known wise old man who lived in the deep woods.

The old man respectfully answered his king's summons. The king asked the wise old man to teach the prince to be a good king. The old man accepted the task.

He blindfolded the prince and led him into the deep woods. He took many false turns so as to confuse the prince so he would not know how to return to the palace. After they arrived at the cottage, the old man taught the young prince how to find food, catch fish, hunt, cook, and survive. Then he left the prince alone in the woods. He promised that he would come back in a year.

A year later, the old man went back. He asked the prince what he thought about the woods. "I am sick of them," the prince replied. "I hate it here. I need a servant. Take me home."

The old man merely said, "Very good. That is good progress, but not enough. Please wait here for another year. I will be back to see you again." Then he left.

Another year passed. The old man went back to the woods and asked the prince the same question. This time the prince said, "I see birds. I see trees. I see flowers and animals." His mind had started to accept the surrounding environment, and he recognized his role in the forest. The old man was very satisfied. "That is great progress," he told the prince. "However, it is not enough, and therefore you must stay here for another year." This time, the prince was not even upset and said, "No problem." Once again, the old man left.

Another year passed, and the old man went back again. The old man asked the prince once more what he thought of the woods. "I feel the birds, the fish, and all the animals. I feel that the woods are alive."

This time, the old man was very happy. "Now I can take you home. If you can feel the things happening around you, you will be able to concern yourself with the people's feelings, and you will be a good king." Then the old man took him home.

Big Rocks in a Jar

One day a schoolteacher came to the classroom with an empty jar and many rocks. The rocks were just the right size to fit through the mouth of the jar. He looked at the class and said, "Students, I am going to conduct a demonstration for you. After you see it, I would like you to tell me how this is related to your life."

The teacher placed the rocks, one by one, into the jar till no more rocks could fit in. Then he looked at the students and asked, "Is this jar full?"

Some students replied: "Yes."

"No! It is not full," the teacher said. He took out some pebbles from the desk drawer and poured them into the jar. Soon the empty spaces were full with pebbles. He asked again, "Is this jar full?"

Having learned from the first question, this time they all said, "No, it is not full."

"That's right," the teacher said. He then took out some sand from the drawer and poured sand into the jar till it reached the top. He asked again, "Is this jar full?"

"No, still not full, teacher," they all replied.

"You are right. It is still not full," the teacher said. Then he picked up the water pot and poured water into the jar till it reached the top. He asked again, "Is this jar full?"

"It is now full," all the students replied.

The teacher looked at each student and asked, "Can anyone tell me how this demonstration is related to your life?"

One student said, "It shows you can always find some extra time to do extra things."

"You are correct, but it is not the key point. The key point is if you don't place the big rocks in first, you will not have a chance to put them in later since the space will be filled with pebbles, sand, and water. The space in this jar represents your life, which is limited. If you know what the big rocks of your life are, you should prioritize them instead of ignoring them. I have seen many people, even some who know what the big rocks of their life are, spend a lot of time doing things that are not important and using them as excuses to avoid big challenges. When time passes and they get old, they find they have lost the chance to fulfill their life's big dreams. So, students, if you want to have a meaningful life, decide what your big rocks are and place them first."

Pipeline in Life

There was a village in the 1950s that was nearly one mile from the river, and all its residents had to walk about two miles each time they needed water from it. There was a rich man in the village who asked two twelve-year-old boys, "Would you like to make some money? If you carry the water from the river to my home, I will pay you fifty cents for each bucket you carry."

"Really, Mister?" The two boys were very happy and liked the job.

So, both boys carried water from the river bucket by bucket each day until the water tank in the rich man's home was full. One boy, after earning his money, would find friends and spend it to have a good time. However, the other boy began to think after he worked for a couple weeks, "I think there is a better way to bring the water to the village."

Thereafter, he began to save the money he earned from carrying water. When he had enough money, he would buy plastic pipes. He began to connect the pipes together section by section. Everyone in the village laughed at him and believed it was not possible since the river was nearly one mile away. However, the boy did not pay attention to what they said. He kept buying pipes and connecting them.

Two years later, when the pipe and water wheel from the river began to carry the water to the village, the boy was just sitting there and collecting money selling water. The other boy was still carrying water bucket by bucket.

A Businessman

A businessman went to a train station. He saw a handicapped person selling pencils in a stall. He gave him a dollar as charity and walked on. A minute later, he returned, picked up a pencil, and said, "I am sorry I thought you were a beggar. In truth, you are a businessman."

Many months passed, and one day he returned to that train station where a shop owner greeted him with smile.

"I have been hoping to see you again," the handicapped person said. "You are the first person who treated me like a businessman. Your kind words helped me to see myself as a businessman and you see, I am a real businessman now."

A Child Crosses the Street

There was a child whose mom asked him to go to the nearby store to buy some eggs. Before he left, his mom said, "Remember, be careful! Before you cross the street, you must wait till the cars pass."

"Yes, mom." The boy left. But about ten minutes later, he came back in tears.

"What happened, honey?" the mom asked.

The boy said, "I have been waiting a long time, but no cars came past."

A Cup of Poison

A young martial artist created a style called Fire Dragon after he had learned many techniques from books, movies, and videotapes. He was so proud of himself and believed that he had created the most effective and powerful martial style in the world.

One day, he went to a martial arts summer camp and met an old master. One morning, when this old master was practicing with some students, he went to see the master.

"Honored master," he said, "I have created a martial style called Fire Dragon. I believe it is the most effective and powerful style ever. Do you mind if I apply the techniques and attack you three times?"

The old master wondered what this young martial artist wished to prove.

"OK," the old master said. "You may do so." He stood low with a proper stance and was ready to accept the challenge.

When this young man began to make his fancy and beautiful movements in front of him without paying attention to the distance between the old master and himself, the old master just slapped his face.

Completely surprised by the attack, he took one step back. The old master waited. When the young martial artist charged forward to attack, the master kicked him in the groin. Now, the young man realized he had no sense of his vital areas' exposure.

He did not attack the third time. He simply bowed with frustration and left. He thought if he did not have even the very simple knowledge of safe distance and postures, how could he then create an effective style? He was sad and disappointed.

That evening, he went to the old master's room. Very humbly, he bowed to the old master and asked a question. "Respectable master, please help me with this question. If I have a cup, but it is filled up with poison, what should I do?"

"Young man, why do you think of the cup of knowledge as small? Envision the cup of knowledge as big. Now all you need to do is put more good water in it to dilute the poison."

After listening, the young martial artist's eyes and face were shining. He bowed deeply to the old master. He knew what he should do next.

A Dog and a Wolf

One day a dog met a wolf. The dog asked, "Do you have a house and car?"

The wolf said, "No!"

The dog asked again, "Do you get three meals and fruit every day?"

Again, the wolf said, "No!"

"Do you have someone to play with you and take you for walks on the street?"

The wolf still said, "No!"

The dog looked at the wolf with distain and said, "You are useless. You don't have anything."

But the wolf laughed and said, "I have clarity about the purpose of my life. I have freedom. I have my mate and my pack. But you are just a dog who thinks he is lucky."

A Driver and a Policeman

When a driver came to an intersection, the traffic light had already changed from yellow to red. He thought, "There is no car around." So he sped up and drove through the intersection.

Unfortunately, a policeman caught him.

"Didn't you see the red light?"

"Yes, I did."

"Then why did you run through it?" the policeman asked.

"Well! That's because I didn't see you."

A Forgotten Regret

My friend's mom went out to dump the trash and was hit by a motorcycle. This triggered a heart attack, and she died suddenly. The whole family was full of sorrow, and the children could not accept the truth about what happened.

"So sad that mom did not say a word and left," one child said.

As a matter of fact, their mom had said many things, such as "Take care of your health," "Don't work too hard, sleep more, less drink" in the past. It was they who did not pay attention to mom's advice.

A Glass

When a glass is filled up with milk, people will say it is milk. When it is filled up with water, people will say it is water. And when it is filled up with oil, people will say it is oil. Only when it is empty, people will notice the glass and see the glass.

A Happy Servant

Once upon a time, there was a servant working for a bad-tempered master. It did not matter what the servant did, the master cursed him, beat him, and tortured him. But, strangely, it seemed the servant was always happy and content. One day, a friend asked, "Your master has treated you so badly. Why are you still so happy?"

The servant said, "You see, half of my life I am sleeping. When I am sleeping, I dream I am a king with many servants who serve me kindly and feed me delicious food. Though half my life is suffering, the other half is happy and enjoyable. Furthermore, because of the half-suffering part, I appreciate the joyful part even more.

"Look at my master. He is angry and restless during the daytime and has nightmares every night. He does not even have a second to enjoy his life. My poor master! He needs help."

THE DAO IN ACTION 163

A Hound and a Rabbit

A hound always bragged that he could run faster than any animal. One day, this hound went to hunt together with his master. The master asked the hound to catch a running rabbit since he always bragged about his ability.

After half an hour, the hound returned without the rabbit. The master was disappointed. However, the hound argued, "Master! You should understand that the rabbit was running for his life, and I chased him just for fun. Therefore, there is nothing strange that I could not catch him."

A Performer and His Assistant

One night, right before a great and famous performer made his entrance onto the stage, his new assistant told him his shoelace was loose. The performer thanked him and knelt down to tie the shoelace.

After the assistant left, he knelt down again and loosened the shoelace. A stage helper saw it.

"Why did you tighten up the shoelace and then loosen it again?"

"You see! My next performance is about a sloppy, tired, and drunk person. When the shoelace is loose, it enhances the image of the performance," the performer said.

"Then why did you not tell that to the assistant?"

"Well! He showed his enthusiasm and concern about my appearance with a kind heart. I did not want to destroy this heart. He will find out the truth later by himself."

A Reward for Kindness

One day a schoolteacher was at home, and the telephone rang. A man said, "I am the manager of Elm Bookstore. I am calling because your daughter was caught stealing a book from my store. You must come immediately to take care of this affair."

The teacher was confused. She could see her only daughter watching television. She was thinking the store had the wrong number when it occurred to her what was happening. A girl, not wanting her parents to know about her stealing, gave the store the wrong number.

The teacher knew she could just ignore the call and hang up the phone. After all, it wasn't her child. On second thought, she considered, "This child may be one of my students! Even if she is not, this child must be frightened and worried." She told the store manager that she was on her way.

When she arrived, there was a girl standing in the store with tears in her eyes, and a few adults were reproaching her.

"Please don't frighten her." The schoolteacher stepped forward to hold the girl tightly in her arms.

She paid the fine, and took the girl home.

"If you like to read books, you may just come here and borrow them. I have many books," she said.

Without saying a word, the girl bowed to her and left. She never came around again. The schoolteacher sometimes wondered what happened to the girl, but she never regretted her actions.

One day, her doorbell rang. A young lady stood outside her door with a lot of gifts.

"Who are you looking for?" she asked.

The young lady started to explain, and something in her mannerisms brought back the memory to the schoolteacher. The young lady who once stole a book had grown up and graduated from college. The young lady spoke with tears falling down her face.

"I still don't understand why you saved me that day, but I always wanted you to know it changed my life."

The schoolteacher's eyes turned red with tears. "What would you have done if I didn't come to help you?" she asked.

"I don't know. I was very troubled back then. To tell the truth, I was thinking of killing myself," she replied.

A Rich Man and His Mother

A rich man went to a dentist with his mother. His mother was old and all her teeth were bad. The dentist introduced various kinds of dentures for them to consider. Some were of high quality and expensive, and some were cheap but of poor quality. The mother chose the cheapest one.

The dentist continued trying to convince them to choose the high-quality dentures. He told them they would fit better and be more comfortable. The mother insisted on her original choice. Finally, the dentist gave up and accepted her demand. The mother took out her purse and paid the doctor. They set up the next appointment and left.

After they left, the dentist and all the nurses despised the rich man and thought he was mistreating his mother. An hour later, this rich man returned.

"My mother came from a poor family and will not spend too much money for herself. Please use the best quality of dentures for her when we come back next week. I will pay all the cost, but please keep this secret between us. Otherwise, she will be unhappy."

A Spider in the Web

After the rain, a spider tried to climb from the bottom of the wet web to the top. He kept sliding down, but he kept trying again and again. There were three people who saw this.

The first one felt his life was just like this spider's, that he had never accomplished anything even though he tried hard. He was depressed and frustrated.

When the second friend saw it, he said to himself, "If the spider circles to the edge of the dried web area, he could reach the top using this detour."

However, the third one believed that as long as he kept trying, he would reach the top sooner or later.

A Change of Fortune

Mr. Huang looked around his grand penthouse office. A few days ago, this office and the entire building it was in had belonged to him. Due to the collapse of his stocks, he had lost almost all of his investments. He lost the building to the bank, had filed for bankruptcy to prevent lawsuits, and still had a huge debt that he did not know how to pay back. He felt it was the end of his world.

He took a last look out at his fabulous view of the city then began to clean out his desk. Stashed beneath some folders he found an old bank deposit book. This book must have been there for the past twenty years. He had completely forgotten about this old bank account. He opened the bankbook and saw he had around one thousand dollars in the account.

He laughed to himself. "A thousand dollars?" he thought. "It was not even enough for one night of entertainment."

It was only 2:00 p.m. He still had enough time to go to the bank to see if he could withdraw this money to help with the emergency situation he was in. When he entered the elevator, the elevator serviceman gave him a smile. He had a ten-dollar bill in his hand. He said, "Did you lose this ten dollars? I found it inside a few minutes ago."

"No, I didn't."

"Then it's my lucky day. This ten dollars will buy me a nice dinner," the serviceman said.

"Ten dollars? What's the big deal? It wouldn't be enough for his favorite glass of red wine," Mr. Huang thought to himself.

When he got out of the elevator, he overheard a young couple. "My first royalty check," the boy said as he was opening an envelope. He pulled out a check and said, "Wow! Seventy dollars."

"Now we can go to a nice restaurant, and then maybe go to see a movie," the girl said.

"Hell! It's only seventy dollars. It's not worth getting so excited. It was not even enough to have one meal," Mr. Huang laughed to himself.

When he passed a fruit stand, he heard a woman bargaining with the stand owner. "Please reduce the price of these fruits. How about three dollars?" she said.

"I am sorry, Madam. I can't do that. I would lose money," the owner replied.

Suddenly, Mr. Huang saw himself. He realized that he had been a lucky and fortunate man, but he had not appreciated it. Now his luck was gone.

He arrived at the bank and gave the bank clerk the bank folder. The clerk looked at it and said, "Gosh! This is a very old account. We haven't used this kind of folder for more than twelve years. Please wait."

Mr. Huang wondered if he could even withdraw this money. It was not much, but to him it was very urgent and important now. A few minutes later, the clerk returned.

"Mr. Huang," he said, "with the accumulated interest over the past twenty-five years, you have a total of $3,200. Do you want to withdraw all of it and close your account?"

"Yes!" he replied, then changed his mind. "No," he said. "Please give me only one thousand dollars and keep the rest in my account."

When Mr. Huang stepped out of the bank with one thousand dollars, he was happy. He still had a great future. It was not the end of the world. If he could do it before, he could do it again. "The future is bright and hopeful," he said to himself.

A Weasel and a Lion

A weasel challenged a lion to fight. The lion refused.

The weasel asked, "Are you afraid of me?"

"Of course not," the lion said, "but if I accept your challenge, you will acquire glory for having fought against a mighty lion, and I will receive a bad reputation for having fought against a small weasel."

A Wise Man and Two Hungry People

Two hungry men came to see a wise old man. The old man gave them one fishing pole and one basket of fish. After a short discussion, one of the men decided to take the basket of fish while the other took the fishing pole. The one with the fish ate and enjoyed the fish all at once. With no fish left, eventually he died of hunger. The man who took the fishing pole had to travel a long distance to reach the lake, and before he reached the lake, he also died of hunger.

Another two hungry men came to see the wise old man. Again the old man supplied a basket of fish and a fishing pole. After a short discussion, the men decided to share the fish and travel together to the lake. The fish gave them nourishment for the journey, and when they arrived at the lake they caught many more fish and survived.

A Prayer's Request

There was a man who badly wished to win the lottery. He prayed to God, "Oh mighty God, please help me and let me win the lottery!" He prayed day and night.

Finally, God got frustrated. "At least go out and buy a lottery ticket first!" he shouted.

We see a lot of people who have good ideas and big dreams but only talk without doing anything about them. This is not the way to realize a dream.

An Ocean Fish Drowns in a Creek

Once there was a man who believed a fish would be able to live without water. So he caught a big ocean fish and threw him in a small lake. After some time, he caught the fish again and let him loose in a fishpond. In this manner he let the fish do with less water every day. In the end the fish was happy with just a wet cloth on its back.

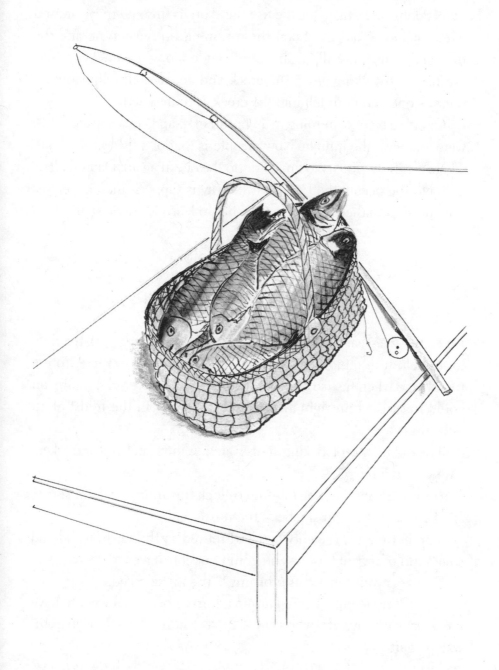

Not long after, he made the fish stand on its fins and move around like a seal or a sea lion. Soon there came a time when he and the fish could enjoy a walk in the countryside along a creek. One day the fish was walking along the creek and accidentally slipped on a mossy stone. The fish fell into the creek and drowned.

Once we were swimming in an ocean of qi and consciousness. We were one with the infinite. Now our life is that of a fish on dry land. There are those who try to find a way to the ocean again. Daoism offers a way to the ocean, the Dao. But the way is slippery and dangerous. One needs a master as a guide. One has to learn to swim again.

An Old Companionship

An eighty-five-year-old man went to a surgeon's office to ask the doctor to help him remove old stitches. The stitches were there from a month ago when he had accidentally been cut. However, the surgeon could not treat him right away because he was in the midst of an operation.

The old man kept looking at his watch. A nurse noticed and asked, "Are you in a hurry?"

"I have an appointment at nine o'clock this morning. I am sorry."

"I can remove your stitches," the nurse said.

The old man was eighty-five and retired so the nurse wondered what kind of urgent business he could possibly have.

"What is your hurry this morning?" the nurse asked.

"I am sorry to bother you. I am in a hurry I because I want to have breakfast with my wife, who is in a nursing home. " He looked at his watch again.

"There, finished. The stiches are out and the cut has healed nicely. You better leave quickly, or you will be late."

"I guess it is OK to be a little bit late. She has had Alzheimer's disease for five years already, and some days she doesn't even recognize me. If I missed one day, it's possible she would not even know. But I would know." He got up and left the office quietly and slowly.

After he left, the nurse said to herself, "This is the love I want. Not faking, sweet talk, or giving me expensive gifts. Real love is priceless and tastes sweet forever."

An Old Man Loses His Shoe

An old man was on the train with his new shoes. The shoes were loose and comfortable. However, as he was walking from one section of the train to another, he lost one of his shoes and it fell to the ground. The train was already traveling at full speed, and it was impossible for him to retrieve his lost shoe.

He quickly took off his other shoe and threw it out of the train. A passenger saw him do this and asked, "Why did you throw out your shoe? You have lost one already."

"You see, I know I cannot get that shoe back so the remaining shoe is useless. By throwing the remaining shoe out, perhaps someone may pick up both shoes and use them."

Annoying Disturbance

A housewife was cooking dinner while her husband stood next to her. As he watched her, he said, "The fire is too high. Cook it slower. You have put too much oil in the pan. Pick up the fish quickly before it becomes a mess."

A few minutes later, the husband continued giving instructions.

"Be careful about frying the vegetables. Not too long and not too short."

His wife was upset. "How can I cook a good meal with all of your interference?" she asked.

"Now you understand what it feels like when I am driving. Please keep quiet so I can drive carefully and peacefully."

Body of Millions of Dollars

A person always complained that he was so poor. One of his friends said, "You have more than one million dollars in your body. Why do you say you are poor?"

"What do you mean? I don't have any money," he replied.

"OK. Will you sell your arms to me for a half-million dollars?"

"No! Of course not," he replied.

"Will you sell your legs to me for another half-million dollars?" his friend asked.

"Don't be ridiculous. I will never sell you my arms or my legs."

"See! You have already have more than one million dollars' worth of parts in your body. Why do you complain? Remember, your body is the most precious and valuable thing you have. Take care of it and do not abuse it," his friend concluded.

Buying a Puppy

A child went into a pet shop when he saw a sign that read "Puppies for Sale." He asked the shop owner, "How much do these puppies cost?"

"In the range of thirty to fifty dollars."

The boy took out a jumble of money from his pocket. He counted out twenty dollars and thirteen cents.

"Can I take a look at them?"

The shop owner whistled and called, "Madam!"

A dog came out from the back, and following her were five small puppies. Four of the puppies were running next to their mom and the last one was limping slowly behind.

"What happened to that puppy?" the boy asked.

"He was born with a defect. The veterinarian said he would be like this his whole life."

A big smile came across the boy's face. "I want to buy this puppy," he said.

"If you want this puppy, I will give him to you for free."

The boy looked straight into the owner's eyes and said, "I don't want him for free. I will pay the same price as for other puppies. I will pay you twenty now, and after that I will give you one dollar each week."

"You really don't have to pay for him, boy! He is not normal like the others."

The boy squatted down and rolled up one leg of his long pants to reveal the deformity of his right leg. It had a metal frame to support it.

"I know what it's like. I can't run like other boys, so I know this puppy will need special care."

The owner's eyes filled with tears. "I sincerely wish every puppy could have a wonderful master like you."

Catch One Each Time

There was a girl who always finished last in the track races at school. From the time of her birth her body had always been weak, and she always had trouble with physical activities. This made her very depressed. Soon, she disliked her physical educational classes. Her mom encouraged her and said, "Instead of trying to catch up to the whole group during a race, why don't you just catch up to the one right in front of you?"

Next time in class, she tried very hard to catch up to the person directly in front of her. To her surprise, she did it and for the first time ever, she did not place last. This victory encouraged her to keep trying.

At the next physical education class she tried even harder. She caught up to two of the people in front of her. This encouraged her to keep trying even harder. She would run on her own, and slowly she built up her strength and stamina. She kept doing better. Along with her body, she built up her confidence.

She applied the same method to all her classes: mathematics, physics, English. When she graduated from school, she was in the top ten of her class.

Choosing a Wife

A rich man was looking for a wife. There were three candidates. He gave each one of them one thousand dollars and asked each one to buy something to fill up a room.

The first candidate purchased a lot of cotton and filled up only half the room.

The second one purchased a lot of balloons and filled up two-thirds of the room.

The third candidate bought some candles and filled up the entire room with light.

The man chose the third one.

Friend and Enemy

There was a bird migrating to the south for warmer weather. On the way, the weather abruptly changed and became very cold. He was frozen and fell onto a field. He waited to die.

A cow passed nearby and dropped dung on him. He began to feel warm and revived. He was so happy lying down in the warm dung that he began to sing.

A cat passed by and heard the singing. He tracked the sound and found the bird. He pulled the bird out of the dung and ate him.

Not everyone who dumps dung on you is your enemy, and there's no guarantee the one pulling you out of the dung is your friend. When you survive a critical situation, you better keep yourself quiet till you are safe.

God's Gift

God invited all the animals to dinner. After dinner, he told everyone, "I have a gift I would like to give to you."

Then he brought out a pair of wings and placed them on the ground.

"If you like it, you may pick it up and put it on your shoulders."

When all the animals stepped forward and saw the heavy wings on the ground, they looked at one another. They thought, "Who will be so stupid to carry these heavy things on their back?"

After they finished looking, they returned to their seats. However, there was a small bird who stepped forward. He believed God's gift must have some use. Therefore, he put the wings on his back and soon he was able to fly. They were not heavy at all. They were so light and could carry him to the sky.

When the animals saw this, they regretted that they did not pick them up.

Good Marriage

Two women were chatting in a cafeteria. One asked the other, "How is your son? Is he OK?"

"Don't even mention it. What an unfortunate thing! His wife is so lazy and does nothing. My son has to work, clean the house, cook the meals, and wash laundry. All she does is watch TV and sleep late. My son has to serve her breakfast in bed."

"Then, tell me, how is your daughter?"

"She has a very good husband. Her husband does not want her to cook, clean the house, wash laundry, or take care of their child. He even serves her breakfast in bed."

Increase the Height of the Fence

People from all around the world have come to take my seminars. This is a story a person from Australia once told me.

One day a zookeeper found that the kangaroos had escaped from their enclosure. After a meeting with his staff, they decided to increase the height of the fence from six feet to ten feet. However, the kangaroos still escaped. Again, after more discussion, the zookeeper gave the order to increase the fence from ten feet to fifteen feet. But the next day the kangaroos were once again found outside their enclosure.

A giraffe next to the kangaroos' boundary asked, "Do you think they will increase the height of the fence even more?"

"It is hard to tell. If they continue forgetting to close the gate, they may."

Losing Money

If you lose one hundred dollars somewhere, will you spend two hundred dollars and your time to find it? Of course you will not. However, people do this all the time. We are often disappointed by others or by situations we cannot control but hang in there for a long time trying to "fix" things. For example, if someone takes advantage of you, you may spend a long time and lots of energy to get even. Is it worth it?

There will be many unhappy events in your life. Will you carry them on your shoulders for a long time, or will you be able to forget them and move forward in your life? Is it worth carrying it?

Lucky Table

Daniel's restaurant was losing customers to the new restaurants opening in his area and he was near bankruptcy. He used to have long lines of customers waiting outside his door before these competitors entered his territory. One morning, he decided to close the business.

That evening, the restaurant had only two guests, a father and a young boy. They ordered one dinner and shared it with each other. A few minutes later, a gentleman wearing a sad expression entered the restaurant.

Daniel looked at the man and thought he might just offer this man a surprise to cheer him up. After the gentleman ordered his meal, Daniel said, "You are the lucky guest tonight. You are sitting in the lucky seat. Your meal will be free, and you will be treated to a special dessert."

The gentleman could not believe he was so lucky that night.

After dinner, Daniel brought him the dessert. The father sitting with his son looked back with a smile. His son said, "Dad, I want dessert too!"

"Where are my manners?" Daniel asked. "I forgot to tell you, for tonight only, we have two lucky seats. Your meal is also free and it comes with dessert."

The small group started chatting. The sad gentleman's name was Frank and he owned a small company. The father's name was Henry. When asked what he did, Henry said, "I was an employee of a small import-export company. However, because of poor economic conditions, I will be laid off at the end of the month. After that, I don't know what I'll do."

"Well! My company is looking for a helper. Would you be interested? If you are, you may come to my company for an interview tomorrow." They arranged the time for the interview.

That night, with his hope about life renewed, Daniel decided to extend his business for one more week and offered a secret lucky table each day. When the news of the restaurant's promotion spread, more and more people came to test their luck. The business soon picked up again. Daniel and Frank had also become good friends.

One day, Frank asked Daniel, "Do you know what I was thinking the first night I stepped in your restaurant?"

"I don't know, Frank."

"Actually, I decided to have a nice dinner and then end my life. My wife had fallen in love with another guy and decided to divorce me. I loved her so much and suddenly felt there was no meaning in life. However, when I sat at the lucky table and then met Henry and his son, I believed that I might still be useful and acquire some good luck. Your generous spirit and helping Henry opened my eyes to a new life."

New Year's Present

On one New Year's Eve, a father and his three daughters sat down to supper. The father drank a goblet of wine then looked at his daughters and said, "As is customary, I am going to give you presents. They are not very precious, but each of you will have the opportunity to show how worthy you are."

He then gave them each a very small package. When the girls opened their packages, they found three copper coins in each one. The daughters thanked him for the presents. The father bid them good night and went to sleep.

When they were alone, the oldest daughter said, "Our father has become avaricious. He could have at least coddled his daughters by offering them silver coins on New Year's Eve."

"What can we do with three copper coins?" asked the middle daughter, shrugging her shoulders.

The youngest said, "Each of father's presents are valuable, and the wisdom hidden in his words is of greater worth than the presents themselves. One only has to understand it."

The following year, at the New Year's Eve supper the father gave each of his daughters a multicolored, embroidered silk girdle. As if he had forgotten about it, he did not mention the previous year's present.

The next year, at the New Year's Eve supper the father asked, "Dear daughters, what did you do with those copper coins I gave you two years ago?"

The oldest daughter laughed and said, "Ah, father, there is no sense in mentioning those three sweets I bought with those three little coins."

The middle daughter got angry. "Why talk about them? I immediately forgot about those little coins. I put them somewhere, and I cannot find them now."

"Father," the youngest daughter said, "I bought a heifer."

"How could you buy a heifer with three copper coins?"

"First I bought a small yellow duckling, which became a beautiful duck. The duck laid eggs that I sold during the year. With the money, I bought a piglet, and when he became big and fat, I sold him. I got enough money to buy a calf. The calf has grown up and become a heifer. In the near future I am going to have a cow, bought with three little coins."

Dream Come True

One day a mouse came upon a deep rice container. He scurried in, and his only thought was that he had plenty of food to eat. So he ate and slept, and ate and slept. Many days passed, and the level of rice became lower and lower until it was near the bottom of the container. He thought, "I still have a lot of rice to eat."

So he kept eating. When he finished the last grain of rice, he realized he could not get out of the container. He died of starvation.

Paid by the Sound of a Coin

There once was a beggar who was so poor that all the money he received was just enough to buy some bread to keep him from starvation. Every day, he would take his bread and sit outside a restaurant. He sat near the door and closed his eyes, smelled the beef or lamb stew, and imagined he was eating it with his bread. He had a nice meal every day.

One day, the restaurant owner caught the beggar sitting outside the restaurant. He accused him of stealing the aromas. He took the beggar to the court. After the judge heard the case, he said to the beggar, "You are guilty of stealing the aromas of his stew. How much money do you have?"

"Your honor," he said, "I have only these few pennies."

"OK. Give them to me," the judge said.

The beggar gave the judge his last few coins. The judge took the coins and faced the restaurant owner. He threw the coins in the air and, when they hit the ground, they made some sounds. He looked at the restaurant owner and said, "Now, you've heard the sound of these coins. You have gotten your payment. Get out of my courtroom."

Priest's Prayer on the Roof

Once there was a big flood. A priest rushed to the roof of his house. The height of the water had nearly reached the roof and continued to rise. The priest got to his knees and prayed to God for a miracle.

Soon a boat passed by. The passengers saw the priest and called for him to come aboard. But the priest said, "No, no, you go on. God is going to save me." So the boat left.

Now the water was past the roof. Another boat passed by and the people called for the priest to get in. But again the priest said, "No, no, you go on. God will save me with a miracle." The boat left.

A few hours later the water rose over the priest's head and he died.

When the priest arrived in heaven, he came before God and was very angry. He shouted, "Why did you ignore my prayer for help?"

"How can you say I ignored you?" God said. "I sent you two boats!"

Psychological Healing

One day a surgeon operated on a cancer patient. His goal was to try to remove the tumor. After he opened the patient's body, the surgeon realized the tumor had spread too far. He could not remove it without jeopardizing the patient's life. So he closed up the patient's body without removing the cancer. The doctor tried to explain but the patient was an uneducated farmer. He could not understand the doctor's explanation. The farmer thought that after the operation, he should be cured. The doctor released the farmer from the hospital.

A year later, the patient went back to see surgeon for a checkup. There was no trace of cancer cells in his body. The surgeon was so surprised that he decided to study psychology and the influence of the mind on healing.

Plot against Plot

A handsome young man sat in a coffee shop waiting for his friend. A beautiful girl came toward him.

"Are you the person my aunt wants to introduce to me?" she asked.

Even though the young man was not that person, he said, "Yes. Please sit down."

On the day of their marriage, he confessed that he was not in the coffee shop for a blind date. His new wife said, "I was not there for blind date either. I was just looking for an excuse to talk to you."

Retirement of an Old Carpenter

There once was an old carpenter preparing to retire. His boss asked him to build one more house before he retired. Though the old carpenter agreed to do so, it was not willingly. His mind was no longer in carpentering. He used poor-quality materials, and his work was rough and unfinished. When he completed the house, his boss told him how much he appreciated his work over the years and that the house was a gift for his retirement.

Selling Milk

A person went out to buy some milk for the weekend. He saw a milk vendor in the street and asked for the price. The vendor said, "If you buy one bottle, it is three dollars, but if you buy three, it will be ten dollars."

After he heard this, he took three dollars and bought one. He then repeated this three times and spent nine dollars to buy three bottles.

He said to the vendor, "Ha! Ha! Did you see that? I just spent nine dollars for three bottles."

However, the vendor replied, "Ha! Ha! I've always seemed to sell three bottles each time after I began this marketing strategy."

The Contented Fisherman

A rich businessman went for a vacation on an idyllic tropical isle. Strolling down to the docks one day he saw a fisherman he knew, comfortably sitting next to his boat and smoking his pipe. The businessman was disgusted.

"Why aren't you out fishing?" asked the businessman.

"Because I caught enough today," answered the fisherman.

"Why don't you fish for more than is needed?"

"Why would I do that?"

"You would earn more money," answered the businessman. "You could have a better engine on your boat and be able to reach deeper water to catch more fish. Soon, you may be able to buy a better nylon net to catch more fish and make more money. Finally, you may become as rich as me: rich enough to buy a new boat—or even a fleet!"

"And then what would I do?"

"You could sit down and enjoy your life."

"What do you think I'm doing now?" the fisherman said.

The Dog and the Reflection

One day a large dog stole a delicious piece of bony beef from the kitchen and was running off with it as fast as he could. He came to a stream and started to trot across the plank that bridged the two banks. He looked down into the clear, quiet water and spied another dog who also had a juicy piece of beef.

STE

"Ho!" said Master Doggie to himself. "What's this? A dog with a piece of beef down there! And a much bigger piece than mine! I'll take it from him!"

He opened his mouth to seize the beef from the dog in the water. Down plopped his own dinner with a loud splash. The ripples cleared, and there, staring up out of the water, was the dog with jaws as empty as his own!

The Love of a Child

When a father returned home after a long day of tiring work, his five-year-old son was at the door to welcome him.

"Dad, may I ask you a question?"

"Of course, son. What is the question?" the father replied.

"How much money can you earn in an hour working for your company?"

"That's nothing you need to worry about, son," the father replied solemnly.

"Please, dad! I just want to know. I am curious," his son said.

"If you really want to know, it is twenty dollars per hour," the father replied.

"May I borrow ten dollars from you, dad?" the boy begged with his head bowed low.

The father was angry. "You want to borrow ten dollars of my hard-earned money? I suppose it is to buy useless toys. I am disappointed in you. Go to your room and think about the whole thing."

The boy went to his room quietly. Later, the father thought he might have been too strict with his son. He was usually such a good boy and didn't ask for much. He went to the boy's room and knocked on the door. "Are you sleeping, my boy?"

"No, I am awake, dad."

"I am sorry I was angry with you. I was tired. Here is your ten dollars."

The boy was very happy. "Thanks, dad," he said.

He then took out another ten dollars from underneath his pillow.

"Why did you want ten dollars since it seems you have ten dollars already?"

"Because I did not have enough. Now, I have enough. Can I buy one hour of your time? Please come home one hour early and have dinner with us. Can you, dad?"

Now the father's heart was touched.

The Love of a Few Dollars

Peter worked very hard. He was so busy he seldom had time to go to see his mom. When he thought of his mom, he would pick up a phone and call her. However, the conversation was often rushed since he was so busy. Sometimes he needed to cut the conversation short due to urgent business. He never knew that his mom just shook her head and sighed with a smile when this happened.

One summer, he had business in his hometown. After he finished his business, he went home to see his mom. When he came down for breakfast, his mom said, "Peter, let's go to the store to buy some eggs."

Peter smiled and thought, "I am the manager of a big company. I have a private secretary and a chauffeur. Buying eggs? My secretary can take care of that."

However, when he looked at his mom's eyes, he nodded his head.

"There is a supermarket where the eggs are on sale. It's one dollar cheaper than usual," his mom said.

When they got outside, Peter was going to hire a taxi. His mom stopped him and said, "There is a special bus service to this super-market. It's free."

Peter just smiled and agreed. When they entered the bus, many people greeted Peter's mom. It was apparent that his mom took this bus often. She proudly introduced him to everyone. Everyone greeted him and treated him like their son.

They bought four dozen eggs and walked back to the bus stop. She said, "Peter, the bus should be here in about an hour."

Peter became uneasy and impatient. However, he tried to cover his feelings. His mom began to reminisce and talk about his child-hood, high school, and many joyful moments they had in the past. Soon, one hour passed and the bus arrived.

On the bus, his mom said, "We saved four dollars on the sale eggs today." She was so pleased.

Peter was thinking, "We have spent four hours shopping and saved just four dollars. If I had used this time in my office, I could have made more than two thousand dollars." However, he did not show this on his face.

After they got off the bus, on the way home his mom used the four dollars to buy a watermelon. Once they arrived home, his mom cut a big slice of watermelon for Peter. Peter was tired and thirsty, and he enjoyed this sweet and delicious watermelon very much. His mother was watching him eat. Her eyes were red from tears, and her face was filled with love. Suddenly, this moment felt familiar to Peter.

When Peter was small, his family was very poor. He loved water-melon, but it was a rare treat. His father passed away when he was very young. His mom had to work very hard to support him until he graduated from college.

Now, Peter realized that all his wealth could not compare with the four hours spent chatting with his mom. He felt so much love from his mom.

The Unhappy Barber

Once there was a barber who was visited by a spirit. He heard the spirit ask him, "Would you like seven pots full of gold?"

The barber looked around him and saw nobody. Greed overwhelmed him and he answered, "Yes, yes, I would like to have the gold."

"Go home and you will find them there," the voice said. The barber hurried home. There, he indeed found seven pots of gold; six were full to the top, but the seventh was only filled halfway. He couldn't bear that the last pot was only half full and became obsessed with filling it.

He gathered all the family's jewelry and gold coins and put them into the pot. However, the pot was still only half filled. This drove him to despair. He economized and stinted. He deprived himself and his family of food. He did everything he could. And yet, the pot was still only half full.

Finally, he asked the king to increase his salary. The king doubled the barber's salary, and the barber continued to try and fill the pot. He drew the line at begging. The pot absorbed each coin he put in, but it was still only half full.

The king noticed how miserable and famished the barber was, and he asked him, "What is going on? When you earned less, you were happy and satisfied. Now you make twice as much, and you are worn out and sick at heart. Do you by chance have seven pots of gold at home?"

"Who told you this, Your Majesty?" the barber asked, astonished.

The king started laughing. "It is obvious," he said. "You look like someone to whom the spirit offered seven pots. Once in the past he wanted to offer them to me, but I asked if I could spend the gold or if it was only to be possessed. When I asked that, the spirit vanished. This gold can't be spent. Go, give those pots back now, and you will be happy once again."

Three Small Devils

The old devil saw that people were very happy in their lives. He said to his three minions, "If people are so happy, then we have not done our job. We should interfere with their happiness."

He sent the first minion to disturb a happy farmer. Though this farmer worked hard, he often had only a meager harvest, and yet he was always satisfied and happy. The minion decided to make the land dry and hard. However, the farmer kept working and continued to till the land with all his effort. He was still happy and worked without any complaint. The minion returned to the old devil and reported his failure.

The old devil sent the second minion to interfere with this farmer again. The second minion thought, "My partner made him worker harder, but that did not make the farmer unhappy. I will take his possessions."

So the second minion took the farmer's lunch and water away. When the farmer went to find his lunch and water, he discovered they were gone. He thought, "Someone must be desperate if he took my lunch and water. I hope it nourishes him." The farmer did not get upset. He just sat in the shade of a tree to rest.

The third minion told the old devil, "I have a good way to make his life miserable."

The third minion disguised himself and made friends with the farmer. He taught him better ways of farming and helped him dig a well so he would never lack water. In just a couple of years, the farmer became rich. He gave up his work habits and became lazy.

The third minion went to see the old devil and said, "I have changed his blood to be like that of a pig, lazy and foolish."

While they were talking, they saw a servant bring a glass of wine to the farmer. The servant carelessly dropped the wine and broke the glass. The farmer became very upset, "You are such a stupid fool, such a careless pig."

"My master! I have not eaten since yesterday. I am so hungry that my body is shaking," the servant said.

"How can you eat without finishing your job? Keep working," the farmer said.

When the old devil saw this, he told the third minion, "You are such a genius! You have corrupted his mind. How did you do it?"

"I just let him own more than what he needs. Therefore, he became lazy, greedy, selfish, and cruel."

Two Escaping Mice

One day a farmer and his crew were cleaning out the barn when they discovered a mouse hole. They used smoke to force the mice out of the hole. They saw one, two, three, four, five, six, and seven mice running out. Satisfied they had gotten all the mice out, they started

to seal the hole. It was only then they could see two mice squeezed together and stuck in the hole. They watched the mice struggle out and then instead of running away they circled each other until one mouse caught hold of the other mouse's tail. At that moment the two mice ran away, one still gripping the other's tail. They figured out one mouse was blind and the other mouse guided the way.

When everyone was sitting down together afterward, one person said, "I think these two mice are master and servant."

"Maybe," another person said, "but I think they are husband and wife."

"I think they are mother and son," the third one said.

"Why do they have to have a relationship?" offered the worker who was usually quiet and everyone thought was simple. "Can they just help each other as a friend?"

Now everyone was very quiet.

Two Mice in a Milk Pot

Two mice lived in a barn. On their nightly prowl they found a glass pot on the ground half filled with milk. They climbed up the pot and tried to drink the milk. Sadly, they both fell into the milk. After kicking for five minutes, one mouse gave up and drowned. The other mouse would not give up and kept kicking. After a while, the milk turned into cheese. He then climbed up out of the glass and survived.

Two Radio Stations

There once was a remote small town. The town had only two radio stations. One station always played popular music; the other only reported the weather. The music station attracted a huge audience, and the weather station had only a small portion of the town tune in to listen.

One night, the weather station announced an emergency. Radar was showing that a powerful tornado was heading toward their town. They advised people to be prepared to find shelter. The station's small group of listeners immediately tried to get the message out, rang the alarm, and called the mayor. However, the mayor said, "A tornado has never touched down in our town. This is false news the weather station created to increase their listening audience." He believed this small group of people had been fooled.

When the weather station tried to share the information with the music station, the station manager was interviewing an important celebrity. The receptionist refused to interrupt the interview.

Within an hour the tornado reached the town. The town was flattened and many people died. Today there is no evidence the town ever existed.

A Frog in the Well
(井中之蛙)

Once there was a frog that lived in a well. He had been born there and had spent his entire life there. There were plenty of bugs and plant life to eat, and every morning when he woke up, he sang with

joy. He would look up at the beautiful sky through the top of the well and sing, "How great and beautiful the sky is! I am the happiest and luckiest frog in the whole world."

One day a frog who lived outside the well accidentally fell into it. He saw the frog that lived there and swam over to him. The first frog was looking through the well and exclaiming how wonderful and beautiful the sky was. When the second frog looked up at the little patch of sky visible through the top of the well, he remembered how big the sky looked from outside the well, and he was very sad.

The Wisdom of a Wise Old Man

One day a sixteen-year-old boy went to see a wise old man.

"How can I be happy and also make others happy?" he asked.

The old man looked closely at the young man. Discerning the boy's sincerity, he said, "It is unusual for someone your age to ask such questions. There are many people older than you who cannot see through their mask."

The boy did not show pride or joy at this compliment. He remained humble, his head bowed.

"I have four sentences to give you," the old man said. "First, treat yourself as others."

The boy said, "Does it mean I should treat myself as equal to others? I should not give myself special treatment."

The old man nodded and said, "Second, treat others as yourself."

"Does it mean I should treat others as equal to me? I should not be concerned with just myself, I should also be concerned for others."

The old man smiled and said, "The third, treat others as others."

"Does it mean I should respect other people's privacy and rights? That each one of us has a unique set of emotions and thoughts, and I should respect what they are."

The old man was pleased the boy understood these sentences. He continued.

"Finally, treat you as yourself."

"Does it mean I should not lose my identity? I should respect myself and build my confidence. I should practice to conquer yourself myself."

The old man laughed with satisfaction. However, the boy asked, "How can I achieve these goals?"

"Practice. Use all your lifetime to learn and to experience each sentence," the old man replied.

Later, when this boy became a man, he became known to the public as a wise man. Many young people came to ask him about life. He would offer these four sentences.

About the Author

Dr. Yang, Jwing-Ming was born on August 11, 1946, in Xinzhu Xian (新竹縣), Taiwan (台灣), Republic of China (中華民國). He started his wushu (武術) (gongfu or kung fu, 功夫) training at the age of fifteen under Shaolin White Crane (Shaolin Bai He, 少林白鶴) Master Cheng, Gin-Gsao (曾金灶). Master Cheng originally learned taizuquan (太祖拳) from his grandfather when he was a child. When Master Cheng was fifteen years old, he started learning White Crane from Master Jin, Shao-Feng (金紹峰) and followed him for twenty-three years until Master Jin's death.

In thirteen years of study (1961–1974) under Master Cheng, Dr. Yang became an expert in the White Crane style of Chinese martial arts, which includes both the use of bare hands and various weapons, such as saber, staff, spear, trident, two short rods, and many others. With the same master, he also studied White Crane qigong (白鶴氣功), qin na or chin na (擒拿), tui na (推拿), and dian xue massage (點穴按摩) and herbal treatment.

At sixteen, Dr. Yang began the study of Yang-style taijiquan (楊氏太極拳) under Master Kao Tao (高濤). He later continued his study of taijiquan under Master Li, Mao-Ching (李茂清). Master Li learned his taijiquan from the well-known Master Han, Ching-Tang (韓慶堂). From this further practice, Dr. Yang was able to master the taiji bare-hand sequence, pushing hands, the two-man fighting sequence, taiji sword, taiji saber, and taiji qigong.

When Dr. Yang was eighteen years old, he entered Tamkang College (淡江學院) in Taipei Xian to study physics. In college, he began the study of traditional Shaolin Long Fist (Changquan or Chang Chuan, 長拳) with Master Li, Mao-Ching at the Tamkang College Guoshu Club (淡江國術社), 1964–1968, and eventually became an assistant instructor under Master Li. In 1971, he completed his MS degree in physics at the National Taiwan University (台灣大學) and then served in the Chinese Air Force from 1971 to 1972. During his military service, Dr. Yang taught physics at the Junior Academy of the Chinese Air Force (空軍幼校) while also teaching wushu. After being honorably discharged in 1972, he returned to Tamkang College to teach physics and resumed study under Master Li, Mao-Ching. From Master Li, Dr. Yang learned Northern-style wushu, which includes bare-hand and kicking techniques as well as numerous weapons.

In 1974, Dr. Yang came to the United States to study mechanical engineering at Purdue University. At the request of a few students, Dr. Yang began to teach gongfu, which resulted in the establishment of the Purdue University Chinese Kung Fu Research Club in the spring of 1975. While at Purdue, Dr. Yang also taught college-credit courses in taijiquan. In May 1978, he was awarded a PhD in mechanical engineering by Purdue.

In 1980, Dr. Yang moved to Houston to work for Texas Instruments. While in Houston, he founded Yang's Shaolin Kung Fu Academy, which was eventually taken over by his disciple, Mr. Jeffery Bolt, after Dr. Yang moved to Boston in 1982. Dr. Yang founded Yang's Martial Arts Academy in Boston on October 1, 1982.

In January 1984, he gave up his engineering career to devote more time to research, writing, and teaching. In March 1986, he purchased property in the Jamaica Plain area of Boston to be used as the headquarters of the new organization, Yang's Martial Arts Association (YMAA). The organization expanded to become a division of Yang's Oriental Arts Association, Inc. (YOAA).

In 2008, Dr. Yang began the nonprofit YMAA California Retreat Center. This training facility in rural California is where selected students enroll in a five-year to ten-year residency to learn Chinese martial arts.

Dr. Yang has been involved in traditional Chinese wushu since 1961, studying Shaolin White Crane (Bai He), Shaolin Long Fist (Changquan), and taijiquan under several different masters. He has taught for more than forty-six years, seven years in Taiwan, five years at Purdue University, two years in Houston, twenty-six years in Boston, and, since 2008 in California at the YMAA California Retreat Center. He has taught seminars all over the world, sharing his knowledge of Chinese martial arts and qigong in Argentina, Austria, Barbados, Botswana, Belgium, Bermuda, Brazil, Canada, China, Chile, England, Egypt, France, Germany, Hungary, Iceland, Ireland, Italy, Latvia, Mexico, the Netherlands, New Zealand, Poland, Portugal, Saudi Arabia, South Africa, Spain, Switzerland, and Venezuela.

Since 1986, YMAA has become an international organization, which currently includes more than fifty schools located in Argentina, Belgium, Canada, Chile, France, Hungary, Iran, Ireland, Italy, New Zealand, Poland, Portugal, South Africa, Sweden, the United Kingdom, the United States, and Venezuela.

Many of Dr. Yang's books and videos have been translated into other languages, such as French, Italian, Spanish, Polish, Czech, Bulgarian, Russian, German, and Hungarian.

Books and videos by
Dr. Yang, Jwing-Ming

BOOKS ALPHABETICAL

Analysis of Shaolin Chin Na, 2nd ed. YMAA Publication Center, 1987, 2004

Ancient Chinese Weapons: A Martial Artist's Guide, 2nd ed. YMAA Publication Center, 1985, 1999

Arthritis Relief: Chinese Qigong for Healing & Prevention, 3rd ed. YMAA Publication Center, 1991, 1996, 2005

Back Pain Relief: Chinese Qigong for Healing and Prevention, 2nd ed. YMAA Publication Center, 1997, 2004

Baguazhang: Theory and Applications, 2nd ed. YMAA Publication Center, 1994, 2008

Comprehensive Applications of Shaolin Chin Na: The Practical Defense of Chinese Seizing Arts. YMAA Publication Center, 1995

Dao De Jing: A Qigong Interpretation. YMAA Publication Center, 2018

Essence of Shaolin White Crane: Martial Power and Qigong. YMAA Publication Center, 1996

How to Defend Yourself. YMAA Publication Center, 1992

Introduction to Ancient Chinese Weapons. Unique Publications, Inc., 1985

Meridian Qigong, YMAA Publication Center, 2016

Northern Shaolin Sword 2nd ed. YMAA Publication Center, 1985, 2000

Qigong for Health and Martial Arts, 2nd ed. YMAA Publication Center, 1995, 1998

Qigong Massage: Fundamental Techniques for Health and Relaxation, 2nd ed. YMAA Publication Center, 1992, 2005

Qigong Meditation: Embryonic Breathing. YMAA Publication Center, 2003

Qigong Meditation: Small Circulation, YMAA Publication Center, 2006

Qigong, the Secret of Youth: Da Mo's Muscle/Tendon Changing and Marrow/Brain Washing Qigong, 2nd ed. YMAA Publication Center, 1989, 2000

Root of Chinese Qigong: Secrets of Qigong Training, 2nd ed. YMAA Publication Center, 1989, 1997

Shaolin Chin Na. Unique Publications, Inc., 1980

Shaolin Long Fist Kung Fu. Unique Publications, Inc., 1981

Simple Qigong Exercises for Health: The Eight Pieces of Brocade, 3rd ed. YMAA Publication Center, 1988, 1997, 2013

Tai Chi Ball Qigong: For Health and Martial Arts. YMAA Publication Center, 2010

Tai Chi Chin Na: The Seizing Art of Taijiquan, 2nd ed. YMAA Publication Center, 1995, 2014

Tai Chi Chuan Classical Yang Style: The Complete Long Form and Qigong, 2nd ed. YMAA Publication Center, 1999, 2010

Tai Chi Chuan Martial Applications, 3rd ed. YMAA Publication Center, 1986, 1996, 2016

Tai Chi Chuan Martial Power, 3rd ed. YMAA Publication Center, 1986, 1996, 2015

Tai Chi Qigong: The Internal Foundation of Tai Chi Chuan, 3rd ed. YMAA Publication Center, 1997, 1990, 2013

Tai Chi Secrets of the Ancient Masters: Selected Readings with Commentary. YMAA Publication Center, 1999

Tai Chi Secrets of the Wŭ and Li Styles: Chinese Classics, Translation, Commentary. YMAA Publication Center, 2001

Tai Chi Secrets of the Wu Style: Chinese Classics, Translation, Commentary. YMAA Publication Center, 2002

Tai Chi Secrets of the Yang Style: Chinese Classics, Translation, Commentary. YMAA Publication Center, 2001

Tai Chi Sword Classical Yang Style: The Complete Long Form, Qigong, and Applications, 2nd ed. YMAA Publication Center, 1999, 2014

Taijiquan Theory of Dr. Yang, Jwing-Ming: The Root of Taijiquan. YMAA Publication Center, 2003

Xingyiquan: Theory and Applications, 2nd ed. YMAA Publication Center, 1990, 2003

Yang Style Tai Chi Chuan. Unique Publications, Inc., 1981

Videos alphabetical

Advanced Practical Chin Na In Depth, YMAA Publication Center, 2010

Analysis of Shaolin Chin Na. YMAA Publication Center, 2004

Baguazhang (Eight Trigrams Palm Kung Fu). YMAA Publication Center, 2005

Chin Na In Depth: Courses 1–4. YMAA Publication Center, 2003

Chin Na In Depth: Courses 5–8. YMAA Publication Center, 2003

Chin Na In Depth: Courses 9–12. YMAA Publication Center, 2003

Five Animal Sports Qigong. YMAA Publication Center, 2008

Knife Defense: Traditional Techniques. YMAA Publication Center, 2011

Meridian Qigong, YMAA Publication Center, 2015

Neigong, YMAA Publication Center, 2015

Northern Shaolin Sword. YMAA Publication Center, 2009

Qigong Massage. YMAA Publication Center, 2005

Saber Fundamental Training. YMAA Publication Center, 2008

Shaolin Kung Fu Fundamental Training. YMAA Publication Center, 2004

Shaolin Long Fist Kung Fu: Basic Sequences. YMAA Publication Center, 2005

Shaolin Saber Basic Sequences. YMAA Publication Center, 2007

Shaolin Staff Basic Sequences. YMAA Publication Center, 2007

Shaolin White Crane Gong Fu Basic Training: Courses 1 & 2. YMAA Publication Center, 2003

Shaolin White Crane Gong Fu Basic Training: Courses 3 & 4. YMAA Publication Center, 2008

Shaolin White Crane Hard and Soft Qigong. YMAA Publication Center, 2003

Shuai Jiao: Kung Fu Wrestling. YMAA Publication Center, 2010

Simple Qigong Exercises for Arthritis Relief. YMAA Publication Center, 2007

Simple Qigong Exercises for Back Pain Relief. YMAA Publication Center, 2007

Simple Qigong Exercises for Health: The Eight Pieces of Brocade. YMAA Publication Center, 2003

Staff Fundamental Training: Solo Drills and Matching Practice. YMAA Publication Center, 2007

Sword Fundamental Training. YMAA Publication Center, 2009

Tai Chi Ball Qigong: Courses 1 & 2. YMAA Publication Center, 2006

Tai Chi Ball Qigong: Courses 3 & 4. YMAA Publication Center, 2007

Tai Chi Chuan: Classical Yang Style. YMAA Publication Center, 2003

Tai Chi Fighting Set: 2-Person Matching Set. YMAA Publication Center, 2006

Tai Chi Pushing Hands: Courses 1 & 2. YMAA Publication Center, 2005

Tai Chi Pushing Hands: Courses 3 & 4. YMAA Publication Center, 2006

Tai Chi Qigong. YMAA Publication Center, 2005

Tai Chi Sword, Classical Yang Style. YMAA Publication Center, 2005

Tai Chi Sword for Beginners. YMAA Publication Center, 2015

Tai Chi Symbol: Yin/Yang Sticking Hands. YMAA Publication Center, 2008

Taiji 37 Postures Martial Applications. YMAA Publication Center, 2008

Taiji Chin Na in Depth. YMAA Publication Center, 2009

Taiji Saber: Classical Yang Style. YMAA Publication Center, 2008

Taiji Wrestling: Advanced Takedown Techniques. YMAA Publication Center, 2008

Understanding Qigong, DVD 1: What is Qigong? The Human Qi Circulatory System. YMAA Publication Center, 2006

Understanding Qigong, DVD 2: Key Points of Qigong & Qigong Breathing. YMAA Publication Center, 2006

Understanding Qigong, DVD 3: Embryonic Breathing. YMAA Publication Center, 2007

Understanding Qigong, DVD 4: Four Seasons Qigong. YMAA Publication Center, 2007

Understanding Qigong, DVD 5: Small Circulation. YMAA Publication Center, 2007

Understanding Qigong, DVD 6: Martial Arts Qigong Breathing. YMAA Publication Center, 2007

Xingyiquan: Twelve Animals Kung Fu and Applications. YMAA Publication Center, 2008

Yang Tai Chi for Beginners. YMAA Publication Center, 2012

YMAA 25-Year Anniversary. YMAA Publication Center, 2009

BOOKS FROM YMAA

101 REFLECTIONS ON TAI CHI CHUAN
108 INSIGHTS INTO TAI CHI CHUAN
A SUDDEN DAWN: THE EPIC JOURNEY OF BODHIDHARMA
A WOMAN'S QIGONG GUIDE
ADVANCING IN TAE KWON DO
ANALYSIS OF SHAOLIN CHIN NA 2ND ED
ANCIENT CHINESE WEAPONS
THE ART AND SCIENCE OF STAFF FIGHTING
ART OF HOJO UNDO
ARTHRITIS RELIEF, 3D ED.
BACK PAIN RELIEF, 2ND ED.
BAGUAZHANG, 2ND ED.
BRAIN FITNESS
CARDIO KICKBOXING ELITE
CHIN NA IN GROUND FIGHTING
CHINESE FAST WRESTLING
CHINESE FITNESS
CHINESE TUI NA MASSAGE
CHOJUN
COMPREHENSIVE APPLICATIONS OF SHAOLIN CHIN NA
CONFLICT COMMUNICATION
CROCODILE AND THE CRANE: A NOVEL
CUTTING SEASON: A XENON PEARL MARTIAL ARTS THRILLER
DAO DE JING
DEFENSIVE TACTICS
DESHI: A CONNOR BURKE MARTIAL ARTS THRILLER
DIRTY GROUND
DR. WU'S HEAD MASSAGE
DUKKHA HUNGRY GHOSTS
DUKKHA REVERB
DUKKHA, THE SUFFERING: AN EYE FOR AN EYE
DUKKHA UNLOADED
ENZAN: THE FAR MOUNTAIN, A CONNOR BURKE MARTIAL ARTS
    THRILLER
ESSENCE OF SHAOLIN WHITE CRANE
EVEN IF IT KILLS ME
EXPLORING TAI CHI
FACING VIOLENCE
FIGHT BACK
FIGHT LIKE A PHYSICIST
THE FIGHTER'S BODY
FIGHTER'S FACT BOOK
FIGHTER'S FACT BOOK 2
THE FIGHTING ARTS
FIGHTING THE PAIN RESISTANT ATTACKER
FIRST DEFENSE
FORCE DECISIONS: A CITIZENS GUIDE
FOX BORROWS THE TIGER'S AWE
INSIDE TAI CHI
THE JUDO ADVANTAGE
KAGE: THE SHADOW, A CONNOR BURKE MARTIAL ARTS THRILLER
KARATE SCIENCE
KATA AND THE TRANSMISSION OF KNOWLEDGE
KRAV MAGA PROFESSIONAL TACTICS
KRAV MAGA WEAPON DEFENSES
LITTLE BLACK BOOK OF VIOLENCE
LIUHEBAFA FIVE CHARACTER SECRETS
MARTIAL ARTS ATHLETE
MARTIAL ARTS INSTRUCTION
MARTIAL WAY AND ITS VIRTUES
MASK OF THE KING
MEDITATIONS ON VIOLENCE
MERIDIAN QIGONG EXERCISES
MIND/BODY FITNESS
MINDFUL EXERCISE
THE MIND INSIDE TAI CHI
THE MIND INSIDE YANG STYLE TAI CHI CHUAN
MUGAI RYU
NATURAL HEALING WITH QIGONG
NORTHERN SHAOLIN SWORD, 2ND ED.
OKINAWA'S COMPLETE KARATE SYSTEM: ISSHIN RYU
THE PAIN-FREE BACK
PAIN-FREE JOINTS

POWER BODY
PRINCIPLES OF TRADITIONAL CHINESE MEDICINE
THE PROTECTOR ETHIC
QIGONG FOR HEALTH & MARTIAL ARTS 2ND ED.
QIGONG FOR LIVING
QIGONG FOR TREATING COMMON AILMENTS
QIGONG MASSAGE
QIGONG MEDITATION: EMBRYONIC BREATHING
QIGONG MEDITATION: SMALL CIRCULATION
QIGONG, THE SECRET OF YOUTH: DA MO'S CLASSICS
QUIET TEACHER: A XENON PEARL MARTIAL ARTS THRILLER
RAVEN'S WARRIOR
REDEMPTION
ROOT OF CHINESE QIGONG, 2ND ED.
SCALING FORCE
SELF-DEFENSE FOR WOMEN
SENSEI: A CONNOR BURKE MARTIAL ARTS THRILLER
SHIHAN TE: THE BUNKAI OF KATA
SHIN GI TAI: KARATE TRAINING FOR BODY, MIND, AND SPIRIT
SIMPLE CHINESE MEDICINE
SIMPLE QIGONG EXERCISES FOR HEALTH, 3RD ED.
SIMPLIFIED TAI CHI CHUAN, 2ND ED.
SOLO TRAINING
SOLO TRAINING 2
SUMO FOR MIXED MARTIAL ARTS
SUNRISE TAI CHI
SUNSET TAI CHI
SURVIVING ARMED ASSAULTS
TAE KWON DO: THE KOREAN MARTIAL ART
TAEKWONDO BLACK BELT POOMSAE
TAEKWONDO: A PATH TO EXCELLENCE
TAEKWONDO: ANCIENT WISDOM FOR THE MODERN WARRIOR
TAEKWONDO: DEFENSE AGAINST WEAPONS
TAEKWONDO: SPIRIT AND PRACTICE
TAO OF BIOENERGETICS
TAI CHI BALL QIGONG: FOR HEALTH AND MARTIAL ARTS
TAI CHI BALL WORKOUT FOR BEGINNERS
THE TAI CHI BOOK
TAI CHI CHIN NA: THE SEIZING ART OF TAI CHI CHUAN,
    2ND ED.
TAI CHI CHUAN CLASSICAL YANG STYLE, 2ND ED.
TAI CHI CHUAN MARTIAL POWER, 3RD ED.
TAI CHI CONNECTIONS
TAI CHI DYNAMICS
TAI CHI FOR DEPRESSION
TAI CHI IN 10 WEEKS
TAI CHI QIGONG, 3RD ED.
TAI CHI SECRETS OF THE ANCIENT MASTERS
TAI CHI SECRETS OF THE WU & LI STYLES
TAI CHI SECRETS OF THE WU STYLE
TAI CHI SECRETS OF THE YANG STYLE
TAI CHI SWORD: CLASSICAL YANG STYLE, 2ND ED.
TAI CHI SWORD FOR BEGINNERS
TAI CHI WALKING
TAIJIQUAN THEORY OF DR. YANG, JWING-MING
TAO OF BIOENERGETICS
TENGU: THE MOUNTAIN GOBLIN, A CONNOR BURKE MARTIAL ARTS
    THRILLER
TIMING IN THE FIGHTING ARTS
TRADITIONAL CHINESE HEALTH SECRETS
TRADITIONAL TAEKWONDO
TRAINING FOR SUDDEN VIOLENCE
TRUE WELLNESS
THE WARRIOR'S MANIFESTO
WAY OF KATA
WAY OF KENDO AND KENJITSU
WAY OF SANCHIN KATA
WAY TO BLACK BELT
WESTERN HERBS FOR MARTIAL ARTISTS
WILD GOOSE QIGONG
WINNING FIGHTS
WISDOM'S WAY
XINGYIQUAN

DVDS FROM YMAA

ADVANCED PRACTICAL CHIN NA IN-DEPTH
ANALYSIS OF SHAOLIN CHIN NA
ATTACK THE ATTACK
BAGUAZHANG: EMEI BAGUAZHANG
BEGINNER QIGONG FOR WOMEN 1
BEGINNER QIGONG FOR WOMEN 2
CHEN STYLE TAIJIQUAN
CHEN TAI CHI FOR BEGINNERS
CHIN NA IN-DEPTH COURSES 1—4
CHIN NA IN-DEPTH COURSES 5—8
CHIN NA IN-DEPTH COURSES 9—12
FACING VIOLENCE: 7 THINGS A MARTIAL ARTIST MUST KNOW
FIVE ANIMAL SPORTS
FIVE ELEMENTS ENERGY BALANCE
INFIGHTING
INTRODUCTION TO QI GONG FOR BEGINNERS
JOINT LOCKS
KNIFE DEFENSE: TRADITIONAL TECHNIQUES AGAINST A
    DAGGER
KUNG FU BODY CONDITIONING 1
KUNG FU BODY CONDITIONING 2
KUNG FU FOR KIDS
KUNG FU FOR TEENS
LOGIC OF VIOLENCE
MERIDIAN QIGONG
NEIGONG FOR MARTIAL ARTS
NORTHERN SHAOLIN SWORD : SAN CAI JIAN, KUN WU JIAN, QI MEN
    JIAN
QI GONG 30-DAY CHALLENGE
QI GONG FOR ANXIETY
QI GONG FOR ARMS, WRISTS, AND HANDS
QI GONG FOR BETTER BREATHING
QI GONG FOR CANCER
QI GONG FOR ENERGY AND VITALITY
QI GONG FOR HEADACHES
QI GONG FOR HEALING
QI GONG FOR HEALTHY JOINTS
QI GONG FOR HIGH BLOOD PRESSURE
QIGONG FOR LONGEVITY
QI GONG FOR STRONG BONES
QI GONG FOR THE UPPER BACK AND NECK
QIGONG FOR WOMEN
QIGONG FOR WOMEN WITH DAISY LEE
QIGONG MASSAGE
QIGONG MINDFULNESS IN MOTION
QIGONG: 15 MINUTES TO HEALTH
SABER FUNDAMENTAL TRAINING
SAI TRAINING AND SEQUENCES
SANCHIN KATA: TRADITIONAL TRAINING FOR KARATE POWER
SCALING FORCE
SHAOLIN KUNG FU FUNDAMENTAL TRAINING: COURSES 1 & 2
SHAOLIN LONG FIST KUNG FU: ADVANCED SEQUENCES 1
SHAOLIN LONG FIST KUNG FU: ADVANCED SEQUENCES 2
SHAOLIN LONG FIST KUNG FU: BASIC SEQUENCES
SHAOLIN LONG FIST KUNG FU: INTERMEDIATE SEQUENCES
SHAOLIN SABER: BASIC SEQUENCES
SHAOLIN STAFF: BASIC SEQUENCES

SHAOLIN WHITE CRANE GONG FU BASIC TRAINING: COURSES
    1 & 2
SHAOLIN WHITE CRANE GONG FU BASIC TRAINING: COURSES
    3 & 4
SHUAI JIAO: KUNG FU WRESTLING
SIMPLE QIGONG EXERCISES FOR HEALTH
SIMPLE QIGONG EXERCISES FOR ARTHRITIS RELIEF
SIMPLE QIGONG EXERCISES FOR BACK PAIN RELIEF
SIMPLIFIED TAI CHI CHUAN: 24 & 48 POSTURES
SIMPLIFIED TAI CHI FOR BEGINNERS 48
SUNRISE TAI CHI
SUNSET TAI CHI
SWORD: FUNDAMENTAL TRAINING
TAEKWONDO KORYO POOMSAE
TAI CHI BALL QIGONG: COURSES 1 & 2
TAI CHI BALL QIGONG: COURSES 3 & 4
TAI CHI BALL WORKOUT FOR BEGINNERS
TAI CHI CHUAN CLASSICAL YANG STYLE
TAI CHI CONNECTIONS
TAI CHI ENERGY PATTERNS
TAI CHI FIGHTING SET
TAI CHI FIT: 24 FORM
TAI CHI FIT: FLOW
TAI CHI FIT: FUSION BAMBOO
TAI CHI FIT: FUSION FIRE
TAI CHI FIT: FUSION IRON
TAI CHI FIT IN PARADISE
TAI CHI FIT: OVER 50
TAI CHI FIT: STRENGTH
TAI CHI FIT: TO GO
TAI CHI FOR WOMEN
TAI CHI FUSION: FIRE
TAI CHI QIGONG
TAI CHI PUSHING HANDS: COURSES 1 & 2
TAI CHI PUSHING HANDS: COURSES 3 & 4
TAI CHI SWORD: CLASSICAL YANG STYLE
TAI CHI SWORD FOR BEGINNERS
TAI CHI SYMBOL: YIN YANG STICKING HANDS
TAIJI & SHAOLIN STAFF: FUNDAMENTAL TRAINING
TAIJI CHIN NA IN-DEPTH
TAIJI 37 POSTURES MARTIAL APPLICATIONS
TAIJI SABER CLASSICAL YANG STYLE
TAIJI WRESTLING
TRAINING FOR SUDDEN VIOLENCE
UNDERSTANDING QIGONG 1: WHAT IS QI? • HUMAN QI
    CIRCULATORY SYSTEM
UNDERSTANDING QIGONG 2: KEY POINTS • QIGONG
    BREATHING
UNDERSTANDING QIGONG 3: EMBRYONIC BREATHING
UNDERSTANDING QIGONG 4: FOUR SEASONS QIGONG
UNDERSTANDING QIGONG 5: SMALL CIRCULATION
UNDERSTANDING QIGONG 6: MARTIAL QIGONG BREATHING
WHITE CRANE HARD & SOFT QIGONG
WUDANG KUNG FU: FUNDAMENTAL TRAINING
WUDANG SWORD
WUDANG TAIJIQUAN
XINGYIQUAN
YANG TAI CHI FOR BEGINNERS

more products available from . . .
YMAA Publication Center, Inc. 楊氏東方文化出版中心
1-800-669-8892 • info@ymaa.com • www.ymaa.com